TO TAME A TYCOON

JUDY ANGELO

The BILLIONAIRE BROTHERHOOD
NOVELLA
Volume 5

THE BILLIONAIRE BROTHERHOOD

THE BILLIONAIRE BROTHERS KENT

Book 1 - The Billionaire Next Door
Book 2 - Babies for the Billionaire
Book 3 - Billionaire's Blackmail Bride
Book 4 - Bossing the Billionaire

THE CASTILLOS

HOLIDAY EDITIONS

Rome for the Holidays (Novella)
Rome for Always (Novel)

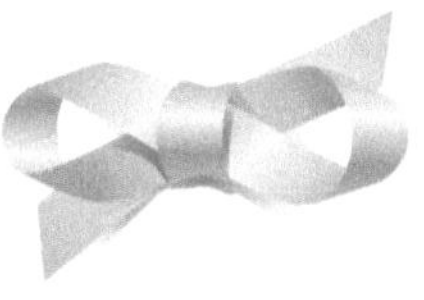

The NAUGHTY AND NICE Series

Volume 1 - **Naughty by Nature**

COMEDY, CONFLICT & ROMANCE Series

Book 1 - Taming the Fury
Book 2 - Outwitting the Wolf
Book 3 - Romancing Malone

THE BILLIONAIRE BACHELORETTES OF BEL-AIR

Book 1 -In Bed with the Enemy

. . ⋙ . .

<u>(More titles at the back of the book)</u>

HOW DO YOU TAME A TYCOON?

ENRICO MEGALOS IS BOLD, brash and a big problem...at least, for his staff in the Miami office of Megalos Shipping. And that's where the lion tamer comes in.

Asia Miller, personality coach, is hired to tame the big boss. She takes on the challenge, not realizing until it is too late that, while taming him, she is also losing her heart...to the one man it doesn't pay to love.

Sun, sea and a steamy affair - a thrilling ride on the sensual side.

CHAPTER ONE

Enrico Megalos. Twenty-seven years old. Probably the youngest shipping magnate in the world. Multibillionaire. CEO of Megalos Shipping and Carinosa Cruise Lines. Of Italian parentage, but grew up in France and did his degrees in Spain. Like so many Europeans, he was multilingual. The man spoke four languages fluently. Impressive!

Asia flipped through the sheets of paper in the file. More details on Megalos shipping. Offices in Miami, Athens and Los Angeles. She shook her head. Megalos had all this wealth and power, and yet his own staff had to reach out to her in desperation. The man needed help.

She gathered the papers together, then slid the whole lot into her briefcase. She had an appointment with Enrico Megalos in forty-eight minutes and she did not intend to be late.

After graduating from the University of Toronto with a PhD in Psychology, Asia Miller had set up her practice as an image and personality consultant, and after only two years in the business, she was sought out by individuals and businesses across the greater Miami area. Enrico Megalos, though, would be her most prestigious client.

Based on the profile she'd received, and the conversation with the human resources director, she knew this assignment was going to be a major challenge, probably the most difficult she'd had to handle so far. Thank God the man had actually agreed to meet with her. Now, it was up to her to make a great impression.

Ten fifty-five found Asia sitting in the luxurious lounge of Megalos Shipping's Miami office. At exactly eleven o'clock a soft-spoken, gray-haired woman came out and greeted her, then escorted her into the inner sanctum, the private office of Enrico Megalos himself.

When Asia walked in, she blinked, caught off guard by the sheer size and opulence of the room. If it could be called a room. The office space looked as large as half of the entire floor. Furnished with exotic pieces that screamed wealth, the place looked like the palatial residence of a prince. And there, standing by the plate glass windows that looked out onto Miami Bay, stood the royalty in question.

As she entered the room, Enrico Megalos stepped away from the window and turned toward her. Asia found herself staring into the deep-set dark eyes of a strikingly handsome man. Tall and lean, he had the poise of a panther preparing to pounce. His jet-black hair glistened in the sunlight streaming through the window, framing his strong, lean face. It was a serious face, with not a hint of a smile to be seen, the tight set of his lips, clear testament to his displeasure.

"Miss Miller." His tone brusque, the business tycoon gave her a curt nod and walked toward her, his movements lithe and smooth. In his designer suit of deep charcoal, he could have been a model on the runway. But if the man was aware of the gorgeous picture he posed, he did not show it. Enrico Megalos was all business.

He held out his hand. "Welcome to Megalos Shipping."

She glanced down at his lean-fingered hands. A pianist's hands, agile and strong, with a latent power that could conquer or caress. She looked up at him, the heat of guilt rising in her cheeks. Now, why had her thoughts gone there? "Thank you, Mr. Megalos," she said quickly, and took his proffered hand.

And that was when something happened. She'd heard about electric shocks and jolts like lightning when there was that special connection between a man and a woman. But...a meltdown? Probably inappropriate, but that was the only word her stricken brain could come up with, in her confusion. She, Asia Miller, all of twenty-seven years old, with a Phd. in Psychology, had simply touched this man's hand, and had suddenly grown moist. Down there. Holy heavens. What was happening to her?

She pulled her hand from his grasp, pretending to brush a piece of lint from her skirt. She needed those couple of seconds to gather her wits about her. She was a professional, here on business. Apparently, her body hadn't received that memo. She would definitely have to rein it in.

"Call me Rico," he said, not seeming to notice her attempt to put distance between them.

"Rico," she said, her voice a breathless whisper. She'd meant it to be a bold statement, a simple repetition of what he'd said. Instead, she sounded like she'd just made love.

"Please. Have a seat." He beckoned toward the chair across from his desk then waited till she'd perched on the seat. Then, he walked over to his desk where, instead of going around it to sit in the chair, he set his bottom on the edge, folded his arms across his suit-clad chest, and gave her a look of impatience.

"Now, Miss Miller," he said, his voice cool, "on the request of my head of HR, I agreed to meet with you this morning. I have a tight schedule today, so let's make this quick. What do you need to know about me?"

His abruptness took her by surprise. No preamble; just straight to the point. No problem. She could be just as direct.

"Thank you for slotting me into your busy schedule," she said, her tone brisk. "Mrs. Haye told me she already spoke to you about why I'm here."

He frowned. "Yes, some horse manure about needing me to tone down. There's a problem with my management style, apparently."

"Yes, Mr. Megalos...Rico...there is." Asia reached down and slid her briefcase onto her lap. She unzipped it as she spoke. "Your management style is very upsetting to your staff. They cannot function in an environment where their leader shouts, pounds his fists on the table and uses swear words."

"No-one's complained," he growled, obviously put out by her plain speech.

"Not to you, they haven't. But there have been several complaints to your HR department." Asia shook her head but smiled in an attempt to lighten her next statement. "If you were an employee, you would have been let go already. Unfortunately, your team can't fire the owner of the firm, so they called me."

For the first time since she'd entered his office, Rico Megalos smiled. "And you have the magic formula to change me?"

"I hope so," she said, responding to his smile. "I've made a name for myself in this business. As a personality coach, I've been able to help a lot of people, and I think I can help you, too."

"How?"

"I won't try to change you, Rico. You will have to change yourself."

"And what if I don't want to change?" His voice was full of challenge.

"Oh, by the time I'm done with you," she said quietly, "you will."

Rico Megalos gave her a look of disbelief. Then, his eyes narrowed. Obviously, he was not used to being challenged. His staff members were probably too scared of him to do anything but jump at his command.

Asia gave an inward chuckle. With her on the case, all that would change. Little did he know what lay in store.

"I've been doing a bit of research about you," she continued, "but I'd like to ask you some questions. I need to understand where you're coming from."

Rico uncrossed his arms and planted his hands on the desk. "You do know this appointment is only thirty minutes long. And I'm not going a minute over that."

"Not a problem. Let's get started." Asia pulled out her notepad and pen. "From my research, I learned that you're Greek by birth, but you grew up in France. Correct?"

"Wrong." He sounded smug. He was probably glad she'd messed up on that first point. "My father is Greek; my mother is Spanish. I was born in France and grew up there but spent summers in England."

"Okay," she said, dragging out the word as she scratched out her line of notes and scribbled down what he'd just said.

"And what does that have to do with anything?" he demanded.

"A lot, actually." She kept her tone cool and nonthreatening. She had no intention of putting him on the defensive. "You have a mixed European background, but now you're in an environment where you must relate to an American staff."

"So?"

"There's a cultural divide here, one which you have to cross. And that's what I'm here for - to help you make that leap."

Rico gave a snort of derision. "You book an appointment and tie up thirty minutes of my day to tell me this? *Merde!* This is all Psychology nonsense." He got up from the desk and walked over to the window. He shook his head, looking tense and frustrated. "Listen, Miss Miller-"

"Asia," she said, calmly watching him, assessing his every move.

"Asia," he repeated. "I don't have time to waste. Europeans and Americans aren't all that different. Our cultures are quite similar. Why waste time discussing my cultural background? It's irrelevant."

Asia shook her head and gave him a gentle smile. "That's where you're wrong. Family background and culture have everything to do with the issues you're having right now."

"I'm not having any issues," he said, his tone defensive. "The employees are."

Asia nodded. "I agree. But as long as they're having issues, you are, too. The head can't be okay if the body is in trouble."

That silenced him. For the moment. As he stared back at her, he frowned, seeming deep in thought.

Before he could come back with a rejoinder, she continued. "Now, let's look at the cultural aspect of things. From my personal observations, I think it is safe to say that Europeans, particularly the French, tend to be more direct in their speech, than Americans."

He said nothing, but cocked his head to one side, and gave her a sidelong glance. He was listening, but he didn't want to seem too interested. She knew that look. At least. he was paying attention. And looking cute while doing it.

Asia shook her head. *Focus, woman.* She continued. "The manner in which you communicate with your team is very different from the norm in this country."

"What manner are you talking about?" He was frowning again.

"You express your anger very openly," she said, keeping all judgment from her voice. "You're free with your expressions of frustration, and often use swear words during discussions. Using swear words is your own personal touch but such behavior does not sit well with the recipients of those reprimands."

"But it's all part of the discussion," he said, looking at her like she was stupid to even bring it up. "How else can you get new ideas if you don't have spirited discussions?"

"Spirited discussion is great." She nodded in agreement. "However, it gets difficult when the boss dominates the discussion and is so free with his judgment and criticism that his team members are driven to silence."

He opened his mouth to speak, but she put up a hand.

"No, let me finish." She was not about to let him dominate her, too. "It may be out of self-doubt, or it may be out of fear, but the fact remains that your people are not talking. They're not sharing their ideas, and it's because of you."

He was biting his lips now, and she could see the struggle on his face. He wanted to speak, but he was not about to let her halt him again. Clearly, he didn't like being told what to do.

"Your leadership style needs a touch of diplomacy, Rico. Sometimes, it's not what you say, but how you say it."

"*Zut alors!* That is enough." He threw up his hands, finally letting out his frustration. "Do you think my people are stupid? Why would they be afraid of me? Just because I let off steam and express myself in meetings? That is hogwash. *Basura.*"

"So, why do you think they called me in?" She gave him a tight smile.

"I don't know," he said. "Probably a stupid joke; just something to waste my time. *Demonios*!"

"Rico," she said softly, "you do realize you've been using swear words in my presence, even though we've just met?"

"Swear words?"

"Yes, swear words. Whether in French, Greek or Spanish, that's what they are - swear words. And whatever the language, they sound just as ugly."

That seemed to take him aback. He shook his head as if he couldn't believe what she was saying, then he walked over and pulled out the chair from behind his desk. He sat down.

When he looked at her, his lips were tight, but his eyes had lost some of their fire. Just a little. "What do you want from me?"

Good. Now she had him exactly where she wanted him. It had finally sunk in, and he was beginning to realize the error of his ways. "I want you to allow me to coach you for the next few weeks, no questions asked. I don't want to make you who you're not, but I want to make you the most effective leader you can be, for your American team."

She got up then, confident in the power she had to help this man, if he would let her. And, for the moment at least, he was ready to listen. "If I am to work with you, I need you to follow my instructions."

That got her a glare, but she pressed on. "To the letter. No objections. And I want to start with this meeting you say you have in less than ten minutes. I want to be in that meeting. I need to see you in action, to observe you as you interact with your various departments. This will be my starting point."

He expelled his breath in a whoosh and sat back in his seat. He did not look at all pleased at her demand. He looked like he was about to object, but then he shook his head. "All right," he said, with a deep sigh. "The quicker you get started the quicker I can get you off my back." He turned his narrowed gaze on her. "You can attend my meeting, on one condition."

"Which is?" She raised an eyebrow at him.

"I don't hear a peep out of you. Not a word, or else you'll be out of there so fast, you won't know what hit you."

For a moment, she just stared at him, letting the silence speak for her. His comment really did not merit a response. He was simply resorting to his tried-and-true technique of intimidation. But he was trying it out on the wrong person.

Asia gave Rico a warm smile, making it clear that she was immune to his threat. "I'm ready for the meeting," she said, deliberately avoiding mention of his comment. "Lead the way."

For a moment, Rico just stared at her, seeming nonplussed. He'd probably expected his nasty comment to get some sort of rise out of her. He was trying to put her on the defensive. She knew that tactic all too well, and it wasn't going to work. Not on her.

As Asia got up from her chair, ready to follow Rico to his meeting, she smiled to herself. This assignment was definitely going to be fun.

Enrico Megalos would soon find out that he had finally met his match.

CHAPTER TWO

*Z**ut*. Rico marched down the hallway toward the conference room with Asia Miller close on his heels. What the heck had he gotten himself into? When Cynthia Haye, his head of HR, had met with him to discuss the little 'problem' in the office, he'd been surprised. He couldn't imagine that his employees were taking his little tirades seriously. Still, when she'd expressed the concern, he'd agreed to meet with the consultant, just to humor her. He'd had no idea that the consultant would have turned out to be a dark-eyed, ebony-haired pixie who looked like she took her job very seriously.

He'd been shocked when the immaculately dressed woman, her hair pulled up into a sleek bun, walked into his office, looking little bigger than a child. She was probably all of five feet three inches tall - in heels. But despite her diminutive size, he could see she was no pushover. When he'd tried to bully her, she'd refused to be intimidated.

But it was when he'd reached out to shake her hand that he had gotten his greatest shock. Their hands touched and, right at that moment, he went hard. Rock solid. Like a damn teenager, with a schoolboy crush. *Merde*.

Now, he would have Miss Asia Miller in his meeting, watching his every move. He would have to be on guard. There was no way he was going to let this 'personality coach' catch him in a faux pas, no matter how beautiful she was.

They were the first to arrive, so Rico took the opportunity to seat Asia at the very back of the conference room, and out of his immediate line of vision. Any closer, and she'd be nothing but a source of distraction.

Jim Henessey, the air operations manager, arrived on the dot of eleven-thirty and took up his usual position at the end of the table, on the side opposite to Rico. They nodded in greeting then Jim's eyebrows raised as he caught sight of Asia. His eyes brightened as he gave her a look of interest.

Rico scowled. What business did Jim have, eyeing a woman he didn't even know? He didn't have time to ponder this further, as Sharon Halliday and Nicholas Pringle entered the room, talking animatedly. They were both regional sales managers reporting to Ben Sampson, the director for sales and reservations, who followed behind.

"Rico," Ben said, and walked over to shake his hand. His sales managers nodded to Rico and took up their positions on either side of their boss. Last to come, were Sarah Snow, VP of Marketing, and Kyle Pitt, her marketing research analyst. They greeted Rico and sat opposite the sales team as they always did. There was an ongoing rivalry between the sales and marketing teams, partly driven by their leaders, and partly by the spirit of competition in the office. Each team was always trying to outdo the other. On the sidelines, was operations, making sure the business ran according to plan.

Rico picked up his pen and leaned back in his chair. "Good morning, everyone. Now that we're all here, let me introduce Ms. Asia Miller who will be an observer to our meeting. She's here to make recommendations on how we can enhance...our communication skills."

At his words, Asia gave a nod to the group, but then her sharp, dark eyes returned to him, and in her gaze was a hint of amusement. Rico tightened his lips and was just barely able to keep himself from scowling. The woman was laughing at him, was she? He turned his attention to his team, his mood moving from serious to sour in seconds. He had to regain control of his emotions. From here on, he would just ignore the woman.

The meeting started out on a less than positive note, with Ben giving a sales report that reflected a decline in cruise ship passengers over the last quarter, even though they'd already entered the summer vacation season.

"What's your excuse this time?" Rico demanded. "This is the third quarter in a row."

Ben heaved a sigh. "And, for the third time in a row, Rico, I have to tell you that the best-made sales strategies and customer calls are nothing in the face of this worldwide recession. People just aren't booking cruises the way they used to. Some of our repeat customers are now without jobs. That's the reality-"

"*Merde.* That's no answer to my question, Ben, and you know it. Our competitors are beating the shirts off our backs." Rico gave a hiss of frustration. "What? The recession hit us, but bypassed them?"

"Jeez, Rico, we've gone over this already." A pink flush was climbing up Ben's neck. "You keep ignoring the fact that our target market is the middle class; working folks who rely on jobs for income. Fantasia Lines and Chrysalis Cruises both cater to the luxury market. It's recession proof-"

Rico waved his hand and silenced Ben mid-speech. Then, he turned to glare at Sarah. "What are you doing about this? Isn't it your job to drive the business? Obviously, I can't rely on sales. At this rate, I'll soon be locking up this shop. So, what are you doing to stop the hemorrhaging?"

Sarah started, then she picked up her pen and began to tap it against her notebook. "Well, Rico," she began, her voice sounding high pitched and strained, "as you know, the budget was cut-"

"Don't give me that crap about the budget being cut." Rico almost slammed his palm on the table. He caught himself just in time. "Don't talk to me about what you don't have. Tell me what you're doing with the money you do have."

"That's what I'm trying to do, Rico." Sarah spoke again, her voice stronger this time. "Each time I try to explain, you cut me off. And you do the same thing with Ben. You do it to all of us."

This time, Rico did slam his palm on the table. "Listen, I don't have the time for whining. All I want is your plan of action to turn this ship around. We have to see a return to profit by the end of this quarter. This time, failure is not an option."

Silence. For a moment, Sarah said nothing. She just stared back at him, the tightness of her mouth revealing her anger.

"May I say something?"

All eyes turned to Jim Henessey. "Sarah's right. Every time someone tries to give you information or tries to make you understand a situation, you cut them off. You never listen-"

"*Carajo*! I listen to you all the time." Rico threw up his hands in frustration. "That's why I have these meetings so often, to hear all the problems, issues and reasons why we're losing business. But also, to hear solutions, Jim. Suggestions on how to resolve the problem. And that's what I'm not hearing from any of you." He shoved his chair back and stood up. "And that's what I'm paying all of you for, *n'est-ce-pas*? Solutions."

No-one answered. They all stared back at him in their strange way, as if they were afraid to express their feelings. For the life of him, Rico could not understand why they refused to speak up. When the silence stretched on, he decided to continue. "Sarah, Ben, what about that competition we instituted last year, between the sales and marketing departments? Hasn't that stimulated some creativity on your teams? And Jim, where is the creativity from the operations department? Come on, guys. I need to see results."

It was Jim who spoke again, and his voice was strangely calm. "Rico, since your previous CEO left, and you set up headquarters in this office, you've called these meetings, and they've not been successful."

Irritated, Rico opened his mouth to respond, but Jim kept talking. This time, it was Rico who found himself on the receiving end of an interruption.

"Nobody wants to talk, Rico, so here is my suggestion. Instead of these round table meetings you always call, let's do formal presentations, with charts outlining what each person plans to say. That way, if we get sidetracked with questions or...disturbing comments, we can still get back to the main topic."

"Fine." Rico spat the word out, too pissed to argue with the man. "I don't see the need for all that, but if that's what it will take to get some information out of you all, we'll do it."

"It's what it will take, for us to have our say," Jim said, his eyes unwavering.

"In that case, this meeting is over. I suggest you all decide on a time for these presentations and let me know. Till then, I have work to do." With that, Rico turned and walked out of the conference room, not even stopping to acknowledge his very quiet observer.

He was mad at Jim. The man had made it look like he was the one who'd been disrupting his own meetings. And he'd done it in front of Asia Miller, the hired busybody. He'd looked bad in front of the 'consultant', and he didn't like it. Not one bit.

He was halfway down the hallway to his office, when he was stopped by the voice of the woman in question.

"Rico. One moment, please."

He stopped and heaved a sigh. He did not turn to face her. She would catch up to him soon enough and, of course, she would give him her professional opinion.

She stepped up beside him. "I'd like to accompany you to your office," she said quietly. "We need to talk."

Rico did not answer. He shoved his hands into his pockets and walked on. Just what he needed. Another lecture.

CHAPTER THREE

"I have an assignment for you." Asia said, as she struggled to keep from smiling.

Rico was sulking, and he looked so cute doing it. He was slumped in his chair, his face set like a thundercloud, and he was angry. He was embarrassed, she knew, because she'd seen him at his worst. She knew he'd started off trying to make a good impression. And he'd failed.

"What assignment?" he asked, his voice a grumpy growl.

"Based on my observations," she said, in her sweetest, most charming voice, "you have two main problems. Number one, you let your emotions get in the way, which results in your bullying your employees. Second, you institute systems that have built-in incentives for your departments to work against each other, rather than together."

"What systems?"

"You mentioned a competition between the sales and marketing departments. Such systems foster a rivalry that may not be in your best interest. Research has shown that giving teams a common goal to work toward is far more effective than setting up competitions between them. Hence, my assignment."

"Which is?" Rico growled.

"I want you to come up with a program that will force the sales, marketing and operations teams to work together.

Design it, implement it, and after two weeks, assess it. I want you to report the results to me at the end of the period. I guarantee you'll see a huge difference in the results of your teams' combined efforts."

"Uh, huh," Rico said sardonically.

"Don't knock it, just try it." Asia was not fazed by his sarcasm. "That's your assignment number one. Remember, you agreed to work with me, so I expect you to keep your word. Do I have your commitment?"

She could see the reluctance flit across his face. He wanted to say no, but how could he, when he'd already told her he would fulfill her requirements? He may be a lot of things, but she could sense that he wasn't the man to back out on a promise.

"All right," he said finally. "We'll reconnect in two weeks. And if what you say works, I'll eat my hat."

That made her laugh. "I have a better idea. If my suggestion works, you'll have to agree to my next task, no grumbling, no questions asked."

"That's it?"

"That's it," she said. "Just be prepared to do anything I say, because I know my experiment will be successful."

"And I know it won't," he countered, his look bold and confident, "so I agree."

Asia got up then, her briefcase in hand, but she did not reach out to shake his hand. This time, she wasn't taking any chances, touching him.

"I'll see you in two weeks," she said, by way of farewell.

He got up and walked her to the door, where he held it open for her. This time when they parted, he was smiling.

"I look forward to it," he said confidently, as she walked through the door.

. . ❧ . .

"ROBERT'S ON HIS WAY over," Shelley whispered, as the tall, gangly youth ambled toward them, his jeans threatening to fall off his lean hips, "and you know what he wants…"

Asia's friend and fellow volunteer left the sentence hanging in the air. There was no need to say another word. They both knew Robert, and they were more than prepared this time. He walked up to the counter behind which both women stood, holding long-handled ladles.

"Double on the mashed potatoes?' Shelley asked, with a stern frown. "Triple," Robert said, his thin face glowing, as he gave them a wide grin. "You know I'm a growing boy."

Asia shook her head. "Don't we know it. I've got double portions of chicken for you. And," she looked to the right and to the left then leaned forward, "I've got something in back for you," she said, in a staged whisper. "Half an apple pie."

Robert's eyes shone and his smile grew even toothier. "Apple pie is my favorite. You're the greatest, Asia."

"Hey, what about me?" Shelley gave a perfect pout. It made her look all of six years old.

That made Robert laugh out loud. "I love you, too, Shelley. I wouldn't give you guys up for the world."

He gratefully accepted the plate piled high with food, and rested it on his tray, then headed for the table in the far corner by the window, his usual eating place. There, he sat down and dived into the meal.

Asia couldn't help smiling. She loved to watch him savor every bite of his meal. "That kid's an eating machine," she said, her eyes still resting on him.

"Yeah," Shelley said, with a chuckle, "all six feet five inches of him."

"D'you think they'll pick him for the community center basketball team?"

"They'd better," Shelley said, her voice indignant, "or else they'll have me to answer to."

"Yeah, right," Asia said, rolling her eyes, "as if anybody's scared of your little four-foot eleven self."

"I'm four feet, eleven and a half inches." Shelley glared at Asia and straightened to her full height.

"Still a shortie," Asia said with a laugh.

"And I'm in good company," the smaller woman said, looking Asia up and down.

When Asia moved away to serve the next teenager, she was still smiling. She enjoyed the teasing fun she and Shelley engaged in, each time they met. They'd both started on the same day as volunteers at the youth shelter and community center and had become fast friends. That had been four years earlier, when Asia had been twenty-one and still in university. Shelley, on the other hand, was a widow, and the mother of two teenage girls. But, as tiny as she was, everyone knew she was a no-nonsense woman who spoke her mind, but who was always quick to offer guidance, comfort and love.

Sunrise Community Center was a refuge for the young people in the neighborhood. It was a place where they could escape from the troubles of abusive homes and dangerous streets, and just be kids. The land and the buildings were a donation from a long dead philanthropist, but his legacy lived on in the positive impact the center was having on so many young lives. Here, the kids could play basketball, soccer, squash and tennis and a warm meal was provided each evening, to all who desired it.

Robert was a regular, and one they both loved. At the tender age of eighteen, he'd found himself alone in the world, no longer eligible for the protection and support of the foster care system. He'd found a part-time job on a construction site, but his wages were not enough to cover the rent and provide for his needs. That was where the center came in. He could count on getting one good meal each day, and his entertainment requirements were satisfied with the variety of sporting activities available on the location.

Robert's situation was not unique. Even though some of the users of the facilities were children from working families, the majority were disadvantaged, and this place was their only means of escape. Asia was glad she was a part of their world, a part of the solution to their problems. She made a good living in her consulting business, and made regular donations to the center. Still, nothing was more satisfying to her than interacting with her young mentees. Through her relationship with such a diverse group, she'd learned courage in the face of adversity, perseverance, and patience.

She'd also come to realize the importance of seeing each person as an individual, with unique desires and dreams. You had to see all the kids as seeds of hope, and the volunteers as gardeners who would nurture them and let them grow to their full potential. Some had already blossomed and moved on to better lives, but there were always new ones who showed great promise, who tugged at your heart strings and made you want to give them the world.

Robert was one of them. His greatest dream was to become a professional basketball player, and so he spent hours on the court, practicing long after everyone else had departed. He was dying to be discovered, and Asia prayed that one day he would be. She smiled, as she watched him rake his fingers through his curly blonde hair, and slouch back in his chair, his ritual after a good meal. It was the sign that he was ready for dessert. Where he put all that grub, she could never tell. He was as thin as a pole. It had to be a combination of a naturally high metabolism, daily manual labor, and practice sessions that went on for hours.

As she stared over at Robert, her eyes went out of focus, and her mind wandered back in time to another man who was tall and lean, but older, and with hair the glossy black of a raven's wing. Enrico Megalos. Her renegade mind kept taking her back to him, making her relive every moment she'd spent with him. It didn't matter that all her interactions with him had been on a professional basis only. No, crazy brain that she had, it kept playing back each scene in her head, and each time it ran the movie, it was sexier than the time before.

The movie ran in slow motion, giving her a close-up view of his broad forehead, the thick dark brows, the lashes any warm-blooded woman would lust over, the long, lean nose that spoke of his heritage, and the piece de resistance - the firm, yet sensuous, lips she was dying to taste.

"Who is he?"

"Uh, what?" Asia blinked, dragging herself back to the present, and turned to stare at her partner in the food line.

"Who is he? The guy you're mooning over?" Shelley cocked an eyebrow at her, and her lips trembled like she was trying not to laugh. "This is the first time I've seen you spaced out like that, and it can only mean one thing. You've found a man. Finally."

"I...haven't," Asia protested, but her voice was too weak, too airy, for her statement to be true. She knew it, and she knew Shelley knew it. Or, at least, she could guess very easily.

"Mm-hmm." Shelley rolled her eyes and pursed her lips, looking so comical that Asia burst out laughing.

"I didn't find a man," she said again, her voice stronger this time. "Really, I didn't."

"Tell that to the birds," Shelley said dryly, then turned toward a lone straggler who approached with a tray. She loaded the girl's plate with food, then watched as she headed off to a free table. Only then, did she turn her attention back to Asia. "Girl, I've known you since you were still beating the books on campus. I know every expression on that sweet face of yours. And psychologist or not, you're no good at hiding your feelings." Shelley dropped her ladle back into the mashed potato and reached for a napkin to clean up a blob that had fallen onto the counter. As she wiped, she continued speaking. "What I see is love, honey. No use denying it. You've got a heart full of love."

"But it can't be." Asia shook her head vehemently. "He's a client."

"Ah ha!" Shelley pointed a finger in Asia's face. "I knew it. You've found a man. And thank God for it. You're finally listening to me."

"Shelley," Asia whispered, "that's not how it is at all."

"How is it, then?" She demanded, her hand on her hip.

"Carol, can you come here a minute?" Asia waved a hand at the white-aproned woman who was chatting with the cook. As Carol approached, she began untying her apron. "Can you hold the fort for a while? Shelley and I need a break."

"Sure," Carol said, with a shrug. "Most of the kids have already eaten, anyway. Nothing much to do."

"Thanks," Asia said, then grabbed Shelley's arm and marched her out the back door. Only when they were outside and out of earshot, did she release her.

"Okay, Miss Nosey Parker," she said, "here's the truth, the whole truth and nothing but the truth." She took a deep breath. "I admit it. I know I've been picky, but I've finally found a man who actually...makes my heart race."

Shelley rolled her eyes as she always did, but now, she was shaking her head in what looked like exasperation. "You can't say it, can you?" She put her hands on her hips in classic Shelley pose. "You finally found a man who turns you on. Say it, girl. Come on." Then, she gave her laugh, the one that sounded like a dog yelping. "I found a man that makes my heart race," she said, in a singsong, mocking voice. "Say what you mean. The man turns you on."

"All right, all right," Asia said, looking around. "Will you keep it down? Are you planning to announce it to the world?"

"So, what's his name? What does he look like?" Shelley said, ignoring her plea. "Is he hot? He'd better be. After your everlasting wait, I don't want you bringing me any old-"

"Will you stop?" Asia felt like gagging the woman. Nice though she was, Shelley had no clue about speaking softly. She pulled her away from the door. "I will not, under any circumstances, tell you his name. He's a client."

"Client, schmient-"

"Stop." Asia put up her hand. "All I'm going to tell you is yes, he's hot, and yes, he turns me on. Big time. But there's nothing I can do about it. Not as long as I'm working for him."

"So, quit," Shelley said with a shrug. "Then ask him out."

"I can't do that-"

"Yes, you can. Asia, you are twenty-seven years old, going on twenty-eight. When are you going to find a man and settle down? Those eggs of yours won't be doing much in a few years."

"Oh, Shelley, you're so funny," Asia said dryly. "This, from a woman who had her first child at thirty-four."

"Yeah, but you might not have my kind of luck."

Asia gave a sigh. "I'll be fine." Then, she smiled. "All I have to do is keep my mind on the job, and out of the bedroom."

To Asia's surprise, Shelley reached out and pulled her into her arms. "You're like a daughter to me, Asia. Please don't keep dallying until it's too late. I want you to find a good man and be happy."

Asia wrapped her arms around the little lady and hugged her back. "I will one day, Shelley. I will."

But even as she spoke, she knew that her heart yearned for only one man. Or maybe it was just her body that was doing the yearning, but still...

That man, excruciatingly handsome and lust-inducing, was - sadly - totally off limits for her.

. . ✧ . .

"RICO, WHICH ONE OF these American women plans on making a good man out of you?" Julio slapped him on the shoulder, almost pitching him into the pool.

Rico shrugged away from his older brother's heavy hand and put some distance between then. If he knew anything about his brother, it was that he should never trust him when he was at his most amicable. As a kid, he'd suffered at the hand of a brother who was nine years his senior, and brawny, to boot. How do you defend yourself from a brother like that? You use your wits, and you move damn fast, never letting him get the upper hand.

So, Rico chose to do that now. Never mind the fact that he was in his twenties, and his brother was in his thirties, Julio would think nothing of launching a surprise attack and knocking him over into the pool.

"Don't you worry about that," he muttered, in a tone which was almost a grumble and walked away from the poolside and toward the patio, where his parents sat, Julio's daughter on the lap of the matriarch of the Megalos family. He was still remembering the last stunt his brother had pulled on him, trapping him with a ditsy dame that time when Julio had hosted a bachelor party for his best friend. He'd been doing everything in his power to hitch Rico up with some chick, any chick, just as long as he could gleefully report to their mother that she would soon be able to expect more grandkids.

Carmelita Megalos was a tiny woman, but her body was the only thing about her that was small. In her family, she wielded a power that rivaled that of her husband. Between the sparrow with her snapping dark eyes, and the bearded lion who had fathered the small tribe of three, there was a constant battle for control. To this day, though in their fifties and sixties, they refused to give up the fight for domination.

But it was a loving rivalry that his parents had enjoyed. They'd been like that for as long as Rico could remember, and they would be just as feisty for many years to come.

Prickly as he usually was, Rico could only hope that he would ever have as good a relationship with whoever might make the mistake of falling in love with him, and becoming his wife. His family was forever teasing him about that.

He looked over at his little niece, "Come here, Athena. Come to Uncle Rico," he said, and held out his arms to the two-year-old.

She blinked up at him, then pulled the pacifier out of her mouth. "No," she said, her voice strong, firm and resolute. Then, she closed her eyes, leaned back against her grandma's belly, and popped the pacifier back into her mouth.

Rico straightened, with a sigh. "No-one can deny that she's a Megalos."

Alexander Megalos chuckled. "The only sweet one in the family. Except for your sister, of course."

"Demetria? She's just as bad as the rest of us. She got Mama's Latin spirit and your directness." Rico laughed. "You never have to wonder what she thinks of you."

Alexander laughed, too, but then he smiled and shook his head. "Pity she couldn't have made it on this trip."

"I know," Rico said, with a nod. "But with the baby on the way, it wouldn't have been a good idea. And remember, she has two other kids under three years old. That's quite a handful."

"Maybe next time," Alexander said, and his voice trailed off as he looked out over the pool, obviously deep in thought.

Most likely, his mind was still on Demetria, his middle child, and as Rico and Julio always teased, his favorite. There was a closeness between Alexander and Demetria that her brothers did not question, or even think of resenting. Who could come between a man and his daughter?

The Megalos family - Alexander and Carmelita, along with Julio, his wife and their daughter - had crossed the Atlantic on their mega yacht as they'd done each year since Rico moved to Florida. They would spend a month in the United States, part of the time at Rico's home on Fisher Island, and the rest, visiting relatives in various cities. The matriarch and patriarch were retired and free to roam, and although Julio was running his own shipping business in Greece, he'd decided that time with family came first. He had no hesitation about spending a month away from the office. While he was traveling, whatever needed to be done, could be done remotely.

Rico loved it when the family visited. It was an opportunity to connect with his culture and heritage. Carmelita would fix Greek and Spanish dishes like nobody else could. She loved to cook, and he loved to eat. It was not unheard of for him to gain five, or maybe even seven pounds, during one of their visits. And - his favorite part - whenever she visited, his mother spoiled him.

Rico flopped down in the chair beside Carmelita and stretched his legs out in front of him. He'd enjoyed the outdoor barbecue and now he was full, relaxed and ready to enjoy the cool evening breeze that wafted over the island. His eyes were closed, and he was almost drifting off, when he felt a warm hand on his arm. He opened his eyes to see his mother smiling at him.

"Are you happy here, Enrico?" she asked gently. She was the only one who still called him Enrico. There was a slight crease between her brows, a sign that she was worried.

"In Miami? Of course," he said, deliberately making his tone light. His mother was a very perceptive woman, and you had to be careful, or she'd read you like a book.

"Are you really, *mi hijo*? You are not lonely all by yourself in this great big country?"

"I am fine, *Mamita*. You don't need to worry." He covered her hands with his.

"And what about the girls?" she persisted. "You did not find any American girl you like? You never tell us about a girl over here."

Rico frowned. He should have guessed where his mother was heading with her line of questioning. On every visit, she would find at least one opportunity to ask questions about his love life. She was convinced that he was lonely without a woman, and had even suggested that he return to Europe to find one. She refused to believe what he told her each time - that he was too busy for a relationship right now. She was convinced that, at twenty-seven, her younger son needed to have a woman in his life.

The truth was, he hadn't met anyone who piqued his interest - until now.

As it had done so often over the past couple of weeks, his mind zoned in on Asia Miller. There was just something about her, petite and soft-spoken, yet so direct and fearless, that made her irresistible.

She was different from the women he knew. She actually stood up to him in her own quiet way. He was not used to that, and it had thrown him off balance for a while. But after he'd gotten over his initial shock, he'd found that he liked her style. She was fresh and she was bold. A perfect fit for the Megalos family.

He caught himself. Why in the blazes had that thought crossed his mind? He glanced over at his mother, but she sat serenely rocking Athena on her lap. It was her fault for planting such thoughts in his head.

No, he couldn't blame his mother. Truth be told, Asia had been on his mind ever since they'd parted almost two weeks before. She'd been so spirited, so confident in her tactics to rescue him from himself, that he'd actually agreed to her deal. And, as she boldly stated, her recommended change to his incentive plan had begun working already. That same day, he'd advised the departments of a new program where they would only be rewarded if the overall company benefitted from their efforts. Teams would no longer be rewarded for individual successes.

After only a week, there was a definite change in the tone of the departmental meeting. For the first time in months, Ben reported a reversal in the trend. It had been a phenomenal week, with sales exceeding target by almost eleven percent. And all because a daring young woman – and, admittedly, one who knew her business - had challenged their status quo and provided new perspective on their business culture.

For the first time since Rico had come to the Miami office, he actually observed sales managers and marketing officers sitting in each other's offices, deep in discussion about how they could combine their skills to achieve the greater goal.

The uptight atmosphere in the office had given way to a camaraderie that he had never seen before.

Asia Miller was good at what she did, and he would be the first to admit, he had a lot to learn. On top of all that, though, he had another situation to deal with. The fact was, he was intensely attracted to her and, advisor or not, there was no denying that he wanted her.

So far, he'd kept himself in check, but he was a man who went for what he wanted, no matter the cost. Next time he saw Asia, it would be time to make his move.

"She's asleep."

Carmelita's whisper broke into Rico's thoughts, and his eyes snapped back to his mother.

"Could you lay her in the crib, please?" Gently, she shifted Athena's little body away from hers, and rested her in Rico's arms. "Try not to wake her."

Rico nodded and gathered the precious little bundle close. For some reason, he pictured an infant Asia looking just like this, with dark hair curling around her cherub face. If they had a daughter, was this what she would look like?

Carajo. Was he going sentimental? He'd better get his wandering mind under control, or else his mother would have her wish sooner rather than later. And he wasn't about to take any chances with his heart - not even for the irresistible Miss Asia Miller.

CHAPTER FOUR

"**A**uto what?" Rico stared at Asia as she sat looking cool and crisp in the chair across from him.

"Autogenic training," she repeated, giving him a little smile. "I want to relieve you of all that pent-up anger, teach you how to release it. Then, I'll take you to the next level where you de-stress."

"But I'm not under any stress." Rico folded his arms across his chest. What did this woman think he was? Some kind of kook who needed therapy? "And I don't need anger management training, either."

Asia shrugged. "Maybe you don't, but why not humor me for a little bit? After all, it can't hurt."

"I don't have time for that kind of nonsense." Asia was annoying him now. This was not how he had foreseen their second meeting. He'd planned to compliment her on the success of her strategy, and then when she was mellow with praise, he would ask her out. But with this stink of an idea, she had taken the meeting in a totally different direction.

Asia did not look the least bit perturbed. In fact, she was smiling. "Rico," she said, in that quiet way he had come to know, "may I remind you of something?"

"What?" He snapped, his tone aggressive and totally unapologetic.

"You already agreed to the training," she said, with the lift of an eyebrow. "Therefore, your comment just now has absolutely no bearing on where we go from here."

"I never agreed to any autogeneric training."

"Autogenic," she said, correcting him. "And yes, you did. At our last meeting, you promised that if plan A was successful, you would undertake the next task I assigned to you, no questions asked. I'm sorry, but refusal is not an option."

For a moment, he just sat there, scowling, pissed that she had him by that very sensitive part of his anatomy. Then, he shook his head, defeated. For now. "All right, you got me. I'll do your autogenic thing...but under one condition."

"Which is?" she asked, looking pleased as a prized puss.

"You agree to have dinner with me."

That got her attention. The pleased puss look disappeared, and in its place was a frown. "Did you just ask me out?"

"I did."

"But...you're my client."

"So?"

"So, it would be...unprofessional."

"I'll pick you up Friday evening, seven o'clock. Make sure you leave me your address."

"Did you hear what I said?" She stared at him, a look of disbelief on her face.

"Sure. I just chose to ignore it."

"Ignore...uhm. Mr. Megalos-"

"Rico."

"Rico, we have a business relationship. I can't go out with you."

"Why not?"

"Because," she said, then faltered. "Because you're my client."

"I think I heard that already," Rico said, leaning forward, "and that means nothing to me. Now, what's your address?"

"Sixteen Beaver Street." The words fell from her mouth, then she turned startled eyes to his and bit her bottom lip.

Rico didn't bother to hide his smile. He had that effect on women. Show them who was boss, and they gave in sooner or later. For him, it was more often sooner rather than later and, he was pleased to know, he'd found the key to Asia Miller. Dominate her before she could even try to dominate you.

"Good. Be ready by seven. And wear slacks."

Now, she looked really confused. To her credit, though, she made no objections. Instead, she nodded and looked away and, just for that moment, she looked like a little lost lamb. A lamb he was looking forward to having for dinner.

Right then, he couldn't wait till the work week passed, and Friday evening came around.

• • ❧ • •

"HOW'S IT GOING WITH the love of your life?"

"Shelley, you never stop, do you?" Asia chuckled into the phone.

"Well, I have to check up on you, don't I? So, did you ask him out?"

"No."

"Chicken."

"But he did."

"He did what?" Shelley asked.

"He asked me out."

34

"He did?" she squealed. "That's wonderful. So, when's the big date?"

"On Friday," Asia said, with a sigh.

"For someone who's got a date lined up for Friday night, you don't sound too happy."

"I'm not."

"Now, listen to this girl." Shelley's tone was heavy with exasperation. "What's not to be happy about?"

"I didn't want to go out with him. I can't even explain how I ended up accepting." She inhaled then released her breath slowly. "Let's just say the man is a pro at getting what he wants."

"And he wants you," Shelley chortled. "Sweet."

"Anyway, I know that wasn't what you called about." Asia said, deliberately changing the subject. The conversation was moving into dangerous territory, too dangerous for her liking. "What's up?"

"You know what I always call you about. The center."

"Something wrong?"

"Yes and no," Shelley said mysteriously. "No, because it's not a threat to the survival of the center, but yes, because it's affecting the kids, especially the boys."

"So, what's going on?"

"With schools reopening in September, we're going to lose three of our best volunteers. Grad students heading back to university."

"Don't worry, Shelley," Asia said, trying to reassure her, "we'll find new ones."

"Yeah, but I'll bet they'll be women."

"So? What's wrong with women?"

"Nothing, except that with Frank, Carlos and Trevor leaving, we've only got one male volunteer left. And even more than the girls, it's the boys who need role models."

Asia drew in a breath. "You're right."

"So, I'm roping you in." Shelley's voice was suddenly bright and cheerful. "I'm on a mission to find two good men before these guys leave, and I'm giving you the same assignment. Two good men, that's all I ask."

"They say a good man is hard to find," Asia said, with a sniff.

Shelley only laughed. "I'm not worried. You'll find me one. I just know it."

After Shelley hung up, Asia left the living room and went into her bedroom. She would be going on her date in two days. She might as well glance through her wardrobe and see what she was going to wear.

Slacks, he'd said. Strange request for a dinner date. She was more of a 'little black dress' kind of girl. But slacks, it would be. That was what the master demanded. She smiled and shook her head. Talk about bossy.

She already knew which one she would wear. Basic black, as always. Okay, so she was boring. But it made life easier. Now, all she had to do was find a nice top.

That didn't take long. She wasn't a fussy dresser. In fact, some had called her 'practical' - which was just a kinder way of saying her clothes were boring. But none of that bothered her. Particularly in this case, she was not dressing to impress. In fact, quite the opposite. Although she had accepted his dinner invitation, she wanted to make it clear to Rico that dinner was all he was going to get. If he didn't know it already, he would soon realize that Asia Miller was no idiot.

But when Friday evening came around, Asia did not feel quite so confident. She didn't know if it was butterflies, but there was definitely something flitting around in her stomach.

Wearing a dress of bright red, a perfect confidence booster, she was ready at seven o'clock, as instructed, and when she heard a car pull up in front of the house, her heart gave a flutter. When she picked up her purse from the table in the hallway, there was a slight tremble to her fingers. She paused to draw in a breath, desperately trying to steady her nerves. The last thing she wanted was for Rico to see her sweat.

She put her hand on the knob and opened the front door to a sight that took her breath away. There, in front of her house, stood an all-white Hummer limousine, and standing by the door of this magnificent vehicle, was a uniformed chauffeur. She whispered a soundless 'wow' then stepped outside. She hadn't expected this. Sure, the man was rich, but she'd thought he would pick her up in a nice car, not a limousine. What would the neighbors think? She almost gave a chuckle as she thought of Mrs. Peabody peeping through the curtains to see what was going on. Mrs. Busybody would have been a more appropriate name for that neighborhood watchdog. She would have a lot to talk about tonight.

So, Rico had 'sent' for her, had he? No problem. She was glad he'd not come himself. Now, she would have a few more minutes to gather her wits about her to prepare for battle.

And a battle it would be - not with Rico, but with herself. She was too darned attracted to the man for her own good. *This is business*, she kept telling herself, *this is business*. She'd said it so many times that her mind was finally convinced. Her heart, though, rebellious as it was, would need more convincing.

As the chauffeur nodded in greeting and opened the door for her, she smiled and murmured her thanks, then bent her head to get into the vehicle. And that was when she saw him.

Rico Megalos sat lounging on the luxurious leather seat of the limousine, looking very relaxed, very sexy, and very much the billionaire. He fit perfectly in this environment. He was dressed in gray slacks and a shirt of soft, white cotton that was open to reveal just a hint of his muscled chest. His clothing was casual enough, but it was the way he wore it, that threw her off. So confident, so blasé; no matter what the man was wearing, he still looked like money.

"Aren't you coming in?" There was an amused twist to Rico's mouth as he watched her, still peering in at the door.

To her chagrin, a blush crept up Asia's throat. She could feel it.

"Hi, Rico," she said quickly, trying to hide her confusion. "I didn't expect to see you."

"Oh?" He cocked an eyebrow. "Didn't I tell you I would come to get you at seven?"

"Yes, but...oh, never mind." She got in, and found herself a seat three or four spaces away from her host. As the chauffeur closed the door behind her, she looked around, and the word that came to mind was 'posh'. She'd been inside limousines before, but none like this one. It came with a lighted bar, which was well stocked with a variety of drinks, and glasses of every shape and size. Light ran along the floor beneath her feet, up the walls, and along the top. A huge TV screen covered the back wall, and speakers lined the sides. The car looked like a ritzy party place.

Realizing she was staring, Asia turned her eyes to Rico. "So," she said, deliberately adopting a serene tone, "where are we going?" Her heart was racing like she'd just finished a run, but Rico didn't have to know that.

"You'll see when we get there," he said, and gave her an enigmatic look and a satisfied grin.

She smiled demurely at him then looked away, pretending to admire the view outside the window. So, he'd decided to be mysterious. No matter. She would know their destination soon enough. Right at that moment, her biggest worry was finding something to talk about. She was trapped in this car with a man to whom she was extremely attracted but who she had to keep at a distance. No matter that her mouth had gone dry at the sight of him, she had to remember that he was a client.

"Would you like a drink?" he asked, as he watched her through half-closed eyes.

"Yes, thank you." Her reply was quick, breathless, as she jumped at the chance for something to occupy her hands and her thoughts, anything to keep her from focusing on his closeness - the woodsy fragrance of his cologne, his strong and handsome profile when she viewed him from the side, the way the fine hairs on her forearm rose up each time he moved near. "White wine would be lovely."

When he poured a glass and handed it to her, she took it, almost too eagerly. She had to force herself to wait before lifting the drink to her lips. She was a bundle of tingling nerves and she needed to regain control.

The first sip helped. She released the breath she'd been holding, then took another sip. By her third sip, her heart had begun to slow, moving back to normal pace. She glanced over at Rico and saw that he was checking something on his cell phone. He hadn't been watching her, thank God. There was no way she wanted him to guess how scared she was, to be alone with him.

After a minute, he glanced over at her. "Sorry," he said, and gave her an apologetic smile. "Bad habit." He stuffed the phone into his pocket. "I've got to learn to leave the office at the office." Then, he gave her a sly look. "Are you going to add that to your list of things to train me on?"

That made her laugh. "Of course not. My list is long enough already." And with the laughter, her tension eased, and she was able to slide back into the plush seat, her body and mind beginning to relax.

Within twenty minutes, Asia felt the car begin to slow, until it came to a complete stop. She peered out the window and saw blue sky, blue water and a big, beautiful white yacht bobbing at the end of a dock.

Asia gasped, then turned to Rico. "Where are we?"

"I wanted to take you somewhere where you can let your hair down." He looked pointedly at the customary bun on top of her head. "We're going to have dinner on my yacht."

Asia's heart lurched. Right then, she couldn't say whether it was from fear or pleasure. "Oh, that's...nice." Not knowing what else to say, she forced a smile, and waited for Rico to make the next move.

Her head snapped up as the door opened and she saw the chauffeur standing there, waiting for them to exit. Rico was holding out his hand to help her and, wary though she was, she placed her hand in his. When his fingers, so warm and strong, encircled hers, she dropped her eyes and forced herself to breathe. No matter what, she had to act normal.

That was easier said than done. When she got out of the car, she found herself standing directly in front of Rico, her face mere inches from the V of his shirt and that rippling chest she'd admired from afar. Now, she found herself so close that she could almost feel the warmth of his body, and her nostrils were filled with the freshness of his cologne. She took a quick step back.

"Are you all right?" He reached out a hand as if to steady her.

She shook her head quickly. "It's okay. I'm fine."

He gave her a quizzical look, then he shrugged. "Okay, then. Let's go."

He gave a nod to the driver, then led the way down the pathway of wooden planks toward the yacht. In Asia's eyes, it was huge, probably almost fifty feet long, she would guess. More than impressive.

They were greeted by a tall, somber man in a white uniform. Rico introduced him as Charles Parker, the captain, who would be taking them out onto the water while they dined below.

After they'd helped her on board, Rico took her on a tour of the yacht. With its TV room, bedroom suites and Jacuzzi, it was like a magnificent mansion on water. Their last stop was the dining room. It was here that Asia got her biggest surprise. It was a luxurious room, with a table set for two, on which sat six softly glowing candles. The setting seemed so intimate, that she hesitated. Did Rico have special plans for the night?

She didn't have time to ponder that question. He'd already pulled out her chair and stood waiting for her to sit. Reluctantly, she stepped forward, then sank down onto the soft cushioned seat. She thought he was going to sit, too. Instead, he wheeled a food trolley toward the table. As he lifted the silver domes that covered each dish, the air was filled with a variety of delicious aromas, and her mouth watered when she saw the feast of fish fillet in a creamy sauce, a mélange of steaming hot vegetables, savory wild rice and a basket of warm bread rolls that smelled freshly baked. The lower level of the trolley had soup, salad, an assortment of dressings and, to Asia's delight, a cheesecake.

"My goodness," she breathed. "How are we going to eat all this?"

"One bite at a time," Rico said, with a laugh. "*Bon apetit.*"

Asia had to admit, Rico played the perfect host at dinner. As they sat eating in the soft light cast by the candles, he entertained her with stories of his life in France, Spain and Britain, and of his large Italian family, in which he boasted twenty-one first cousins on his father's side.

"My father has eight siblings," he explained, at her look of shock. He chuckled. "It could have been worse."

Asia could not imagine being part of such a huge family. How did they keep track of one another? Compared to Rico's family, with the collection of intriguing characters and gregarious relatives he'd told her about, her family seemed dull and boring. Both her parents and her eighteen-year-old sister still lived in her hometown of Oakville in Canada; they usually visited her maybe once or twice a year. She also went home each Christmas. A family gathering for them was their household of four people. She had cousins, of course, but combining all those she'd acquired from both parents, she would reach a total of eight. Even so, they rarely had gatherings where they all met. Probably only at weddings and funerals. They were a far cry from the hundred-person parties that Rico told her about.

As Rico sipped his after-dinner cup of coffee, Asia stole a furtive glance at him. No wonder he was the way he was. As a child, he'd probably had to be bold and assertive just to be heard in what must have been a busy and boisterous family environment. She could just imagine the interaction among the cousins, particularly the boys, each trying to outdo the other as they fought for dominance. Rico would have had to be strong and forceful to hold his own.

A smile tickled her lips as she thought of what he must have been like as a youngster in the Megalos family. With his lean figure, he must have been a scrappy little thing, fighting his way past bigger, brawnier boys until he was able to compensate with a height that probably exceeded the majority of them. Rico was at least six foot one, taller than the average man, and that would have definitely worked in his favor.

"What are you thinking?"

Asia blinked. Rico's question brought her back to earth with a bump. "Oh, nothing," she said airily. "Just enjoying my tea." To prove the point, she picked up her cup and took a sip.

"Very good," he said, with a nod. "I'm glad you've enjoyed the meal." Then, he smiled and reached for her hand. "Now, it's time to burn off some of those calories."

"Excuse me?" Her eyes snapped to his, and she made to pull her hand away, but he held it fast. His smile took on a mocking twist. He must have guessed what she'd been thinking. "Let's go for a walk."

Still holding her hand, he stood up, forcing her to rise, and then he turned her toward the stairs leading up to the deck. "Up you go."

He helped her up, following close behind. Up on deck, the cool air of the salty ocean was a contrast to the intimacy of the cabin below.

A light, almost imperceptible shiver ran through her. The light silk of her scarf was poor protection against the night air which had dipped a few degrees since they'd boarded the yacht.

Rico must have seen her involuntary shiver because, before she knew what was happening, he'd gathered her in his arms, holding her so close, she could feel the beating of his heart. As he held her, he stroked her arms which were bare and at the mercy of the night air.

"Let me warm you up," he whispered, as he stroked, his movements slowing to a seductive caress that was making a heated blush suffuse her body. He'd said he'd warm her, and he was certainly doing that...too successfully. She suddenly felt so hot, she was almost panting.

She swallowed. "I'm...all right," she tried to say, but it came out as a weak whisper, then a gasp as, without warning, he dipped his head and captured her mouth with his own.

Dear God, what was happening? She knew, of course. Rico Megalos was masterfully and expertly taking over. He was seducing her, and she couldn't do a darned thing to stop it. She didn't want to.

His lips, so strong and hard in the boardroom, were warm and pliable on hers. He was gentle with his kiss, as if soothing her fear, calming her jangling nerves, filling her mind with nothing but his kiss. Then, as she relaxed into him, reveling in the hardness of his body against hers, he deepened his kiss, sliding his tongue past her lips to explore her even more.

And that was when she knew the battle was lost. He was an expert kisser, teasing and taunting, probing then plundering, until all she could do was cling to him as he swept her away in the seduction of his caress.

Heart racing, nipples taut and tingling, she moaned when he pulled his mouth away to trail his lips down her neck and toward the curve of her collarbone. There, he tempted her with tantalizing kisses, until she arched her back, wanting more of him.

A fire raged in her belly, the flames reaching up inside to lick at the taut tips of her nipples. Oh God, she wanted him. She needed his lips, his tongue, on those tortured nipples. She wanted him to soothe, to quench the fire that threatened to consume her.

"Please," she gasped, and reached up to slide her trembling fingers through the sleek silk of his hair. Without hesitation, he moved his mouth lower. With powerful hands, he lifted her higher, his mouth sliding down to the crevice between her breasts.

He knew what she wanted. Dear God, he knew. Asia arched her back, her body clamoring for more. He answered her plea when he took the top of her bra in his teeth and pulled it down to expose her distended bud to the air. And then, to her sweet relief, he sucked it deep into his mouth, sending a tremor rippling through her body. God, that felt good.

Too soon, Rico pulled his lips away and set her gently on her feet. "You're cold," he whispered. "Shivering. Let's go downstairs and get warm."

Downstairs. Get warm. The words were like alarm bells going off in her head. Her eyes widened as she stared up at him. What the heck was she doing? How could she have been so stupid? She'd lectured herself to death about not getting involved with a client. And then, she'd gone and let him kiss her. And more. And now, he was inviting her downstairs to 'get warm'. Where? In the bedroom? Not in this lifetime.

Asia pulled out of Rico's arms. "I don't think so," she said, her voice as cool as the air wafting in off the ocean. "I think I've had enough for one evening. I'm not ready to be anyone's...entertainment."

Rico dropped his hands and stepped back, a frown darkening his face. "What are you saying?"

"I'm saying, I want to go home." She fixed him with a stare as frosty as her voice. "Now, please."

For a while, he stared at her, saying nothing. Finally, he spoke. "Very well. We will go." Without another word, he turned on his heel and walked away, leaving her shivering in the chill of the sea air.

Slowly, she turned back to the railing and stared out onto the inky-black water. She wrapped her arms around herself, seeking what little warmth she could. As cold as she was, until Rico came back, she would not be moving from this spot. Downstairs, warm and cozy though it might be, was off limits for her.

The fact was, she was weak. The events of the night had demonstrated that very clearly. She was a professional, but she was not acting like one. She was ashamed to think it, but her behavior was more like that of a love-struck schoolgirl. And she'd almost paid dearly for it. Asia sniffed and bit down on her lower lip. From here on, she would keep her emotions in check, no matter the cost to her heart.

That night, the journey back home was total torture for Asia. After such an idyllic day in Rico's company, it was so hard to accept reality. But with the realization of her folly, the euphoria quickly evaporated, and she resigned herself to accept the return to reason. Going forward, while on the job, she would focus on fulfilling the requirements of her contract...and nothing more.

CHAPTER FIVE

"**S**end her in," Rico said into the intercom, then he swung his chair around so that it faced the plate glass windows overlooking Miami Bay. After her rude rejection on the boat, and a silence of over a week, Asia Miller was back. To conduct her autogenic training, she'd said, sounding so cool and composed that he'd felt like reaching through the phone lines to throttle her.

That was some stunt she'd pulled on his boat that Friday night. After what he'd thought had been a wonderful dinner, where he'd seen her relax for the first time, she'd made a U-turn, questioned his motives, and demanded that he take her home. Just like that. As if he were some kind of lecher, taking advantage of her. He hadn't forced himself on her. She'd kissed him back. Willingly. In fact, she'd responded with a passion that made her desire plain as day.

And then, she'd backed away.

Now, she'd returned to continue her cockamamie training program. He'd almost told his assistant to cancel the appointment. But no, peeved though he was, he would see her. He was more than curious to see whether her frigid mood had improved or not.

Asia Miller entered his office a minute later, looking serene as she always did, her hair in that damn bun she seemed to love so much. On the yacht, when he'd kissed her, soft tendrils of her ebony hair had slipped from the bun to curl softly around her face. With her thick black lashes and the cute pout of her soft lips. she'd made a pretty picture. How could he have resisted stealing a kiss?

But now, the thin line of her lips told him she was back to business.

After her initial greeting, she walked over to the table by the window and opened the briefcase. She began to pull papers out. Only then, did she look him full in the face. "We have a lot of work to do today," she said, and waved her hand to an empty chair. "Can you come over here, please?"

He could see that she was trying hard to project a professional image. She probably didn't realize it, but it was spoiled when she kept stealing glances at him, her face going pink each time. Clearly, Asia was nervous.

And it was this that made a question sneak into his mind. Was he being harsh? He'd probably frightened the girl with that kiss. He'd never been one for subtlety. He took what he wanted, when he wanted, and that was just who he was. With Asia Miller, though, he might have to try another tactic, maybe even take it slow. He wanted her. That was without question. But he could see that she wanted to maintain a distance, probably to hold on to her professional image. Well, he could be slow; he could be charming. He could take it easy and give her some time. Then, he would make his move.

Rico walked over and sat in the chair as Asia had instructed. She was opening her mouth to speak but he put up a hand and stopped her. "Before we begin, there is something I'd like to say." He leaned forward and rested his arms on the table. "I'm sorry for the way I behaved the other night and I hope you'll forgive me."

Asia blinked, looking nonplussed. Then, like the lifting of a fog, the tension in her face disappeared. "I...yes, you're forgiven. And...thank you." She fiddled with the papers in her hands. "I hope you understand that...we have to keep our relationship professional. You're-"

"I know," he said, with a dry laugh. "I'm your client."

She nodded, then pulled out a folder and placed it in front of him. "Now," she said, her tone suddenly firm, "this is my plan of action for you. We'll do a session today, and then these are instructions for you to follow each day, for the next two weeks." Gone was the hesitant woman who had walked into his office. The old Asia Miller, the one he'd met on day one, was back.

She shifted the folder to the side then straightened. "Today, we'll practice a relaxation technique that will allow you to relieve stress and achieve balance."

He shrugged. "I'm not under any stress."

"That's what you say, but your body says otherwise." She walked around the table and reached out to press her hand against the right side of his neck. "Look at how your pulse is jumping. You're not calm. You're wound too tight."

At the feel of her fingers on his skin, he almost groaned. If this was her way of getting him to relax, she was off to a poor start. Her touch had the opposite effect. If the sudden tightening in his groin was anything to go by, he had a long way to go before he could be described as relaxed.

"Your tension and stress are reflected in your aggressiveness," she was saying. "And that's why it's so important to address the problem now, rather than later. These things can lead to physical manifestations, such as heart attacks."

He sat up straight, paying attention now. "Hold on. What aggressiveness are you talking about? I'm not aggressive."

Asia smiled and shook her head. "It's okay, Rico. Denial is typical. And that's why I'm here. As a professional, I can point out these shortcomings and help you overcome them."

"But I'm not aggressive. I'm just an assertive person who speaks his mind." He shook his head. " *Merde*," he said, under his breath, "I wish more people would be like that."

"And that swearing," she said, with the lift of an eyebrow, "we'll work on that as well." She stepped back. "Now, I want you to relax the tension in your shoulders. Just roll them forward and let them slouch."

Rico gave a deep sigh, then he did as he was told.

"Take off your jacket. That way, you'll be less restricted." Asia waited patiently as he shrugged off the piece of clothing, then slumped forward again. "Now, say after me, 'my right arm is heavy.'"

Rico almost laughed out loud. What the hell was this? A joke? But a glance at her face told him Asia was quite serious. And she was waiting.

"My right arm is heavy," he muttered, glad nobody from his staff could see him right then. They would think the boss had gone batty.

"My left arm is heavy."

"My left arm is heavy," he repeated.

"My legs are heavy."

"My legs are heavy."

"My body is warm."

"My body is warm." To his surprise, as he chanted the words his body had begun to act on each of the suggestions. He was feeling slow, heavy and unrushed. And he was warm, a cozy kind of warm.

"My face is cool." Asia's voice was low and soothing, and almost seemed to come from a faraway place.

"My face is cool," he repeated.

"I am filled with peace."

"I am filled with peace." By the time he'd got to that line, Rico was almost falling asleep.

"Now, breathe." It was that quiet voice again, Asia's voice, that was prompting him. "Breathe deeply."

He breathed in and out, long, deep breaths that seemed to cleanse him from the inside out. With each breath that he exhaled,, he could feel the tension flow from his body and the stresses slip from his mind. A few more breaths, and his mind went blank.

"Now, listen to me, Rico," said the faraway voice. "Follow my instructions. Arms firm."

It felt like new life was flowing to that part of his body.

"Legs firm."

His legs came back to life.

"Body firm and just right," Asia said, and her voice was closer now, stronger. "I remain at peace."

Rico's head flopped back against the chair, and he looked up at Asia as she stood watching him. He'd never felt so relaxed in his life. And so free. "What did you just do to me?" he asked, as he stared up at her. But he was smiling, because whatever she'd done, had felt good.

"I was getting you balanced," she said simply. "Releasing the anger, relieving the tension, creating a foundation on which you can build strong techniques." She gave his shoulder a light tap. "Sit up and get your jacket on. Now, you're ready to face the day." As he slipped his arms into the sleeves, she continued. "Once you practice the techniques outlined in your folder, you'll be able to de-stress on a daily basis. In fact, I recommend that you start with a balance exercise before you begin each workday."

"If it will make me feel as good as this one just did, no problem." He rolled his shoulders back, then looked at Asia. "Is this what you do each day?"

Asia smiled. "I do it often, especially when I feel I need that extra boost."

"And is that why you're always so calm?" he asked, genuinely curious now. "Hardly anything seems to throw you off balance." Then, he chuckled. "Except my kiss, of course."

He was a bit surprised when she laughed at that one. He'd half expected her to get defensive, maybe even peeved. But no, she hadn't been offended at the reminder. Her dark brown eyes sparkled as she laughed, and her pink-painted lips curved up in a sweet smile that made him want to kiss her again. Right here. Right now.

He leaned toward her. "I want to see you again, Asia." He was watching her face, gauging her reaction to his request.

Her smile slipped away, but she nodded. "You will. Two weeks from today I'll do a follow up session with you."

"You know what I mean, Asia. I don't need to spell it out." He leaned back in the chair. "But I know your principles and that's why I agree to stay away from you until this coaching contract is completed. After that, I'll no longer be your client, so there's nothing that should get in the way of my asking you out." Then. he thought of something and asked, "Is there?" He gave her a pointed stare.

"No," she said quietly. "There isn't."

"Good. I'm glad that's settled."

"Thanks for being such a good student today," she said, as she buckled her bag.

"I actually enjoyed it," he said, and reached for the folder. "I'm looking forward to trying out some of these exercises of yours."

She looked like she was ready to go but he stopped her. "One last question," he said. "Once I do these two weeks of exercises, I'm done with the training, right?"

"That depends," she said, giving him an enigmatic look.

"On?"

"On whether you pass the final test. If you don't, I'll have to give you another two weeks of work."

"What?" He hadn't contemplated the possibility of anything delaying his completion. What if he didn't pass the test? He had no intention of waiting four weeks before he could invite Asia out again.

"What's on the test?" he asked. "How can I prepare?"

"Sorry, can't tell you." She was shaking her head and grinning at him. She must have guessed his worry because she seemed to be enjoying torturing him with the possibility of failure. "It's an impromptu test. You won't know when it's coming, the nature of the test, nor how it will be graded. Let's just say, if you're ready to go back into the conference room, I'll know."

"Well, that's a big help," he said, with enough sarcasm for her to tut-tut at him. "Whatever it is, Miss Asia Miller, I will pass that test," he declared. "Failure is not an option."

She bowed her head, then bid him goodbye and went through the door.

After she'd left, Rico got up and grabbed his car keys from the desk. He had a meeting with the shipping association in half an hour. It had been a sore point on his list of things to do for the day, but now he felt ready for it.

And in two weeks, he would be ready for his second date with Asia Miller.

$\cdot\cdot\;\approx\;\cdot\cdot$

HE WAS GOING TO MAKE it. She could just tell. Darn.

Was it unfair of her to be secretly wishing for the failure of her own client? Or was she just being a chicken? Maybe Shelley was right - she was running 'man-scared'. Maybe her trepidation had little to do with Rico's being a client. Maybe she was just scared of the man himself.

She shook her head. What the heck was wrong with her? It was her job to tame this tycoon. That was what the corporation was paying her for. So, how could she be scared of him?

Snap out of this, Asia, and get started on a plan to tame the social side of this beast. You're the one with the PhD in Psychology. Not him. Now, come on. Start acting like it.

After that pep talk to herself, Asia felt ready to meet 'the client'. Two weeks had passed since she'd given Rico his stack of assignments, and now it was time to assess his progress. She'd started out wishing that he would fail, just to buy herself those extra two weeks before she would have to worry about his invitation. But no, she would go into this meeting wishing him the best. She was a professional, and she would not let personal desires take precedence over professional responsibility. Whatever the outcome, she was ready.

When Asia arrived at the offices of Megalos Shipping, she did not go immediately to Rico's floor. Instead, she stopped in to see Cynthia Haye, the woman who had hired her.

"Welcome, Miss Miller," the woman gushed, and ushered her into her office. "It is so good to see you."

Asia smiled as she entered the room. "I assume that means you have good news for me?"

"Please. Please, sit." The woman pulled a chair out and waved her visitor into it. Then, she bustled around the desk that looked much too large for her. "I don't know how to thank you," she began. On her face was a broad smile and she looked eager to share her good news. "I have never in my life seen such a dramatic change in a person. And a change in a positive direction at that."

"What have you observed?"

"It started some weeks back, with the revised incentive program with the departments." Cynthia put her pen to her lip, looking thoughtful.

"We started seeing an upswing in sales, and with that, an improvement in Rico's mood. That's easy enough to explain, I guess. But then, this past week, something about him changed." She frowned. "I can't quite put my finger on it, but all I know is, instead of scowls, we're getting smiles, and instead of roars of anger in the conference room, we're actually having discussions." She turned a confused face to Asia. "What in the world did you do to him?"

Asia laughed. "I simply gave him a greater awareness of group dynamics, and then I provided him with an outlet for his tension. It's simple. All he needed was balance."

"Well, however you got him to that state of balance, all I can say is, we're grateful. Staff morale has shot up to a point I've never seen before." Then, she leaned forward and spoke in a loud whisper. "I don't think anyone will be leaving Megalos Shipping for a long time. We'll probably have to pry them loose with a crowbar."

That made Asia laugh. Still, she would give the human resources director one last chance to tell her where the coaching session had fallen short. "He can't be perfect, though. Are you sure you don't want me to observe him in another meeting?"

"Of course, he's not perfect. But considering where he's coming from, he's an angel now. We'll take him the way he is."

So, there it was. That part of her relationship with Enrico Megalos was over and done. Now, to face - and take control of - phase two, the social side.

"I'm pleased that you're satisfied with my work," she said, as she stood up and shook Mrs. Haye's hand. "If you need any further assistance, you know where to reach me."

"Of course, Miss Miller." She walked Asia to the door and held it open for her. "And I will be recommending your services to my business associates. You can be sure of that."

After thanking her, Asia headed down the hallway toward Rico's office, where she would hold her final conference with him, an exit interview of sorts.

She stopped by his assistant's desk, and when she was ushered in, it was an uncharacteristically calm Rico who she saw. And he was without a tie. Looking casual and ultra-sexy in jacket and a shirt open at the collar, he seemed more relaxed than Asia had ever seen him before.

As soon as she sat down, she gave him the good news. "Congratulations. You've passed the test. You're ready to fly."

"Well, that was quick. You take one look at me, and you give me a passing grade. I thought I'd at least have to do some multiple-choice questions."

"This is your lucky day," she said. "I got some overwhelmingly positive feedback about you, and on the strength of that, I've decided to let you loose."

"Perfect," he said, leaning back in his chair. "Now, with nothing restricting you, we can make the arrangements for our next..." He paused, seeming to be giving his words some thought. "...date. Wear jeans or shorts."

She paused too, feeling guilty. She knew it was her fault he'd hesitated. Then, she decided to jump in. "Trousers again? Where to? Another of your yachts?"

"No, a sailboat."

"A sailboat?" Asia's eyes widened in horror. "I don't want to go on a sailboat. What if it capsizes?"

"You can swim, can't you?"

"Yes, but that's besides the point."

"Okay, since you're the guest, you can have a choice," Rico said. "Sailboat or motorboat? Which do you prefer?"

"Motorboat. As long as we don't go too far from shore."

"Motorboat it is, then," Rico conceded, "although I can't fulfill your second request about not going too far from shore."

"Why not?" Asia asked, a twinge of worry creeping into her mind.

"Because I want to take you to my private island on the outskirts of the Bahamas."

"I...don't think I like the sound of that." What did he think she was? Crazy?

"Don't worry about it now," he said gently. "We'll talk about it when I pick you up Sunday morning at seven, okay? I'd like to get an early start."

What part of no, did this man not understand? Before she could refresh his memory that she was in disagreement, he said something which silenced her, at least for the moment.

"Relax, Asia. You'll be in good hands. Just imagine that your whole body is heavy. Relax and breathe." Then, he gave her a mischievous grin.

Oh, no. The man had turned autogenic expert, giving her a taste of her own medicine. Under the circumstances, the only thing she could do was laugh.

CHAPTER SIX

On Sunday morning, Asia was up with the rising sun. She was actually looking forward to spending the day with Rico. Now that their professional relationship was over, she could let her hair down. Literally. Today, she would forget the bun, and let her hair fall loose around her shoulders. He'd said she should relax, and she planned to.

Now, if only she could control those rebellious butterflies that refused to settle down. She wasn't even sure why they were there. Was it because she was scared of going on a motorboat, or because she was scared to be with Rico? Or both? She drew in a deep breath then let it out slowly. Then, she closed her eyes in a brief moment of relaxation. She might as well practice what she preached.

When Rico arrived at seven o'clock, she was ready. She'd dressed in jeans and a halter top blouse, but she'd thrown a light jacket into her tote bag, just in case. She remembered how chilly the sea air had been that evening on the yacht. so this time she wasn't taking any chances.

Today, there was no Hummer limousine to startle the neighbors. Rico was driving a Mercedes Benz convertible sports car which immediately put her in a good mood. She'd hated the pomp and glamour of the limousine, but this car was just right.

As soon as she'd hopped into the passenger seat, they set off for the seashore. The wind whipped through her hair, sending it streaming behind like an ebony scarf, making her feel so carefree that she could not help laughing and holding her hands up to catch the wind.

It was a perfect day, and Asia was heady with anticipation. Before, when they'd been on that first boat, she'd been determined to fight her attraction for Rico. Now, though, things were different. Why should she fight something that felt so right, something that was beginning to feel so real?

And it was that thought that tightened the tension inside her. The problem was, she could no longer vouch for herself. If put to the test, where Rico made a move, what would her reaction be?

She still did not know. Therein lay the question. She would just have to play things 'by ear' and hope that she didn't do anything stupid...again.

As they walked along the dock toward the boat, the early morning sun warmed her shoulders and arms, but the breeze from the ocean tempered the rays of the sun just enough that she was comfortable. Cottony clouds floated by, soft-white and fluffy against the brilliant blue of the sky.

On a day like today, how could she be afraid of a boat? The ocean was like a placid aquamarine bedspread, so calm and comforting. She'd been silly to want to stay on shore, when there was so much blue sea to explore.

And, to visit Rico's private island - that would be something. She was looking forward to it.

"*Tu es prete, mademoiselle?*" Rico held out his hand to her.

"Pardon me?" She didn't speak French and couldn't even begin to make a wild guess at what he'd just said. And the way he kept switching languages...how could she ever keep up?

"Are you ready, miss?" He gave her a smile and a bow of the head, his attitude one of such deference that she couldn't help smiling as a wicked thought ran through her mind. Rico Megalos serving someone? With his huge ego and all that money, never in a million years.

"Certainly, *monsieur*," she said, with a smile, and took his hand. She was enjoying this game they were playing. Enrico Megalos, at your service. That was his self-appointed role for the day, and she was loving it.

Rico helped her climb into the motorboat, and she soon realized that it was not half as scary as she'd thought. It was much smaller than the yacht, of course, but at almost thirty feet in length, it was long enough for her to feel safe and secure.

Her captain for the day hopped in beside her and slipped behind the wheel. In baseball cap, polo shirt, and jeans, he looked even younger than his twenty-seven years. The wide grin on his face added to his youthful appearance. She could hardly believe this was the same man she'd met so many weeks before, the one who'd had his face screwed into a permanent scowl. She liked the new Rico Megalos.

"I packed a picnic basket." He turned and reached behind to lift the lid off what looked like a low storage cabinet. Inside was tucked a basket, bottles of wine, bottles of water and a wide-brimmed straw hat. There was even a bottle of sunscreen.

"You'll need these," Rico said, and reached for the hat which he promptly plopped down on her head. "As much as I love your hair, I'm going to have to hide it. I'm here to serve and protect, and sunburn is not an option."

Asia had to smile when she heard him use what must be his favorite phrase. He'd found yet another thing that was 'not an option'.

"And you need this." He reached for the sunscreen and squeezed a dollop into his hand. Then, as casually as if he did this every day, he began to spread the lotion across her shoulders and upper back.

As his hands slid over her body, Asia tried to relax. She really did. But how could she when, with each stroke of his hands, Rico was stoking the embers that had lain dormant down below. Within seconds, his casual caress had those embers glowing, making her want to squirm. Jesus, if the man didn't stop, those embers would burst into flames, and then she would get moist, unable to control her body's involuntary reaction to his expert touch.

"Uh, thanks, Rico," she said, as she shifted in her seat. She didn't want to offend, but she had to get away before she got too caught up in the sensations. "I think I'm good now." She softened her flight with a smile.

"No problem," he said with a shrug, then proceeded to slather his neck and arms.

Thank God he hadn't asked her to do that for him.

He settled back and started the engine. Then, he put on his sunglasses, and they were off.

They shot away from the shore and Asia squealed in delight. It was a new and thrilling experience for her, racing across the ocean in a high-speed boat. Instead of feeling frightened, she felt exhilarated. Thank goodness she hadn't denied herself this fun experience.

"It's just a couple of hours away," Rico yelled. over the roar of the engine. "Just relax and enjoy the ride."

And she did. After a few minutes on the water. he cut the speed to a cruise, and she leaned back in her seat to enjoy the refreshing breeze as it slapped against her face. Her nostrils filled with the salty sea air and tiny water droplets sprayed her face. In the heat of the sun, it felt wonderful.

By the time Rico pointed to his island in the distance, Asia was drunk from sun, sea and wind. She yawned, feeling more relaxed than she'd ever been, even with her therapeutic exercises. It felt so good to be far away from the bustling beehive that was Miami. While other people thought Miami a slow city, it had always seemed busy to her. That was probably as a result of having grown up in a sleepy little town in southern Ontario. No matter, though. Today, she would be chilling on her own private island. Well, Rico's island, but at least she'd be there to share it with him.

Rico reduced the throttle as they approached, then they rode the gentle waves toward the shore.

Asia, captivated by the picture-perfect scenery, could only stare. It was like a postcard from paradise. The white sand of the beach glistened in the sunlight, as if a million tiny diamonds had been scattered all along the shore. The translucent blue sea licked gently at the sandy beach, the water so clear that as it touched the sand it seemed to disappear. As the sea breeze blew inland, the coconut palms bordering the sand waved and bowed as if in greeting.

"Wow," Asia whispered, never taking her eyes off the scene, "it's beautiful."

"Glad you like it," Rico said. "Welcome to my own little island paradise. It's where I go to get away from my world."

Rico directed the boat toward a tiny dock, then jumped out and secured it before turning to her. He reached out a hand to help her out of the boat. Gingerly, she stood up as the boat rocked gently in the water, then she put her hand in his and he pulled her toward him. She hadn't expected such a powerful tug and she toppled forward, almost knocking him over.

Rico laughed and pulled her into him, crushing her against his strong, lean body. "Trying to knock me into the water, are you?" he growled playfully. "That calls for punishment."

Asia's head snapped up. "I wasn't. I just tripped."

That was as far as she got. Rico's head descended, blocking out the rays of the sun, and then his mouth was on hers, punishing her with a sweetness that left her wanting more.

When he raised his head to look down at her, she moaned. If this was the type of punishment he meted out for bad behavior, she would have to misbehave more often.

He gave her a crooked smile. "Great way to start the day," he said, and then he let her go.

As he stepped away, Asia sighed. It had felt so good to be in his arms, even for those brief seconds. And that kiss. It had left her wanting more. But there was hope. He'd said a great way to *start* the day. Did that mean there was more to come? She could hardly wait to find out.

It was funny how the simple fact that Rico was no longer her client had made such a difference for her. Okay, she would be the first to admit that she'd been attracted to him from day one. But still, there had always been that barrier, that one thing that stopped her from giving in to her desire.

But now? She dared not even think about it. She would have to tread very carefully. She wanted him, and that was dangerous.

Rico had retrieved the picnic basket and a bottle of wine. He even had a rolled-up blanket tucked under his arm. "Come on," he said, with a jerk of his head. "Let's go stake out our turf."

Asia giggled. "As if there's anybody else to fight with."

"Well, you never know." He cocked an eyebrow. "There may be some wild beasts who don't appreciate our company."

That brought Asia to a sudden halt. "Are there wild animals on the island?"

Rico looked amused at her sudden fright. He shook his head. "Don't worry. The biggest beasts you'll find are probably birds, turtles and conch."

"Oh," she said, feeling stupid. Of course, he wouldn't have taken her to an island with dangerous predators. She knew that.

Rico set off with his load, leaving Asia to follow. She had to practically run to catch up, his long strides giving him a distinct advantage. When she got close, she pulled the blanket from under his arm. She could at least help him carry that one thing.

They set up camp in the shade of a low almond tree that had spread its arms far over the sand, creating an oasis of cool, crisp air. There they spread the blanket, using rocks to secure all four corners before the wind whipped it away.

Rico plopped down on their makeshift bed and reached out to drag the picnic basket toward him. "Snack time," he yelled, as he lifted the lid and began to offload its contents.

"But we just got here," Asia protested. "I want to explore."

"Sit, woman," Rico growled then he grinned up at her. "I'm starving. I'm not going anywhere until this beast is fed." He rubbed his stomach and, as if on cue, it growled.

"You're hungry already? But we just got here. It's not even eleven o'clock."

"Ten twenty-one, actually," he said, glancing at his watch. "Perfect time for a snack."

Asia could tell it was no use arguing. When she saw that Rico had already placed half the contents on the blanket and had even started munching on a bread roll, she gave up the fight. He was obviously hungry and how could she blame him? He probably hadn't even stopped growing yet.

She chuckled at that thought. Here she was, acting like Rico was way younger than she, when they were actually the same age. Outside of the office environment though, she just couldn't see him as twenty-seven.

But after the meal. Asia was left in no doubt that Rico was no boy, but a mature and virile man, with not an ounce of shyness about him.

They dined on crispy fried chicken with bread rolls and a salad, then lounged on the blanket, drinking a light wine cooler. Rico packed the basket away, saving the potato salad and half of the chicken for later. Then, he told her he was ready for dessert. And it wasn't the sweet and delicious kind.

All her trepidation forgotten, she lay back on the ground - her stomach comfortably full, her eyes barely open, as the hypnotic sound of the wind in the trees threatened to slide her into slumber - when she felt his closeness.

As she lifted her heavy eyelids, he leaned over her, the red, green and gold of the leaves forming a colorful background behind him. He dipped his head, but instead of aiming for her lips, this time he went lower, nipping at her right nipple as it peaked in her halter top.

Asia gasped in shock and pleasure. He'd gone for that oh, so sensitive part, and it left her panting. But he was just teasing, playing, and it was driving her crazy. She wanted more.

Boldly, she raised one hand to cup the back of his head and with the other she lowered the top, exposing the turgid nipple to his gaze. "Suck on it," she ordered.

His eyes went to hers and Asia could see his surprise at her demand. Then, his lips curled in pleasure, and he lowered his head to obey her command. He nuzzled the nipple then slipped it into his mouth and sucked softly and sweetly until she arched her back in ecstasy or agony. Asia couldn't tell which. All she knew was that the caress of his tongue was turning her insides to lava.

Asia tightened her grip on Rico's head, and she pulled down on the other side of the blouse. Her other nipple was ready and eagerly awaiting attention. Gripping the back of his head with both her hands she pulled, none gently, until his face hovered over her breasts, his lips so close that his breath warmed her nipples. She pulled his head down and he opened his mouth to take the distended member into his mouth.

Asia groaned and threw her head back, transported to a place where all she could do was succumb to the waves of euphoria that washed over her. As he pinched and rolled her nipples with her lips and tongue, she clung to him, pressing his face into her breasts, her hand a vise that ensured he could not move away if he tried.

Finally, her breasts soothed, she pulled his head away and applying pressure, she moved his face toward hers. He came willingly and immediately covered her lips with his.

But she wanted more. She wanted to dominate this man, make him understand that she was in charge. In all her interactions with him, she'd been cool, she'd been calm, she'd been collected - the consummate professional. But now it was time to show Rico Megalos the real Asia Miller. She'd had enough of keeping the tigress inside her in check.

With their lips still joined Asia wrapped her arms around Rico and tilted her body, nudging him until he was forced to roll over onto his back. Then she was on top, taking control of the kiss. This time it was her tongue that probed his mouth, tasting then plundering with a passion that left them both panting.

"*Mon Dieu*, who are you?" Rico said between breaths as he stared up at her.

She slid her fingers through his hair and chuckled. "It's still me, Rico, but now I can be free." She looked away from him and out over the stretch of sandy beach. "Out here, it's just you, me and the island creatures. There's no need to be politically correct. Here, I can just be me."

When she looked back at him, a slow smile was spreading across his face. "I'm liking this new Asia Miller," he said, and raised his hand to slide his fingers into her hair. "So bold," he whispered, "and so beautiful." Then, he cupped her head and pulled it down to give her a kiss so full of passion that all she could do was melt into him.

Then, she pulled back, wanting to regain the upper hand. She had to diffuse his arousal, make him relax again, so she could rule. She would try humor. "So, then I'll say, so reckless," and she gave him a peck on the cheek, "and so young."

He laughed at that. "So, we're speaking soap opera now? Please, no. I don't even watch those things."

She put her lips close to his ear. "Maybe you should. You'd be surprised at what you could learn about love."

Rico shook his head and gave her a fake frown. "Are you saying I'm not adequate in the love department? Are you insulting me, Mademoiselle Asia Miller?"

"Not at all," she said, smiling down at him. "I'm just telling you; you have a lot to learn."

"What?" He gave her a look of indignation then his face softened in a smile. "And are you going to be the one to teach me?"

"That depends."

"On what?"

"On whether or not you can follow instructions. To the letter." She gave him a mischievous smile, and when he responded with a look of bewilderment, she couldn't help laughing.

"You know, you are such a-"

"Weirdo?" she asked, cutting him off.

"I was going to say, a mystery. I still can't believe you're the same Asia Miller I met that day back in August."

"I know," she said, with a teasing smile. "Weird, isn't it?"

"No, not weird but...confusing." He tilted his head as he looked up at her. "It's as if, once the bun came down and you let your hair fall free, a totally new Asia was born."

"Well," she said, rolling off him, "the question is, do you like the new Asia." She lay down beside Rico, closed her eyes, and drew in a deep breath of salty air. She almost didn't want to hear his answer. What if he hated who she really was? What if he preferred the demure, unflappable Asia she'd projected for her professional world? She bit her lip and waited, not wanting to breathe till he'd given his verdict.

She felt him move beside her and knew that he'd shifted from his back and onto his side. He was staring down at her. She could feel it. And still, she did not open her eyes.

"Asia," he said quietly. "Look at me."

Slowly, she exhaled, and opened one eye to peer up at him, then the other. She remained silent.

"I love the new Asia Miller," he said. "This is the Asia I want."

He'd said love. Okay, so he didn't really mean love as in, 'in love'. It was just a figure of speech, but still, it had sounded darned good.

The tension in her dissolved and she gave him a wide smile. Then. she began to giggle. She couldn't help it.

He frowned down at her. "Now, don't tell me there's a third Asia Miller in there somewhere, a can't-stop-giggling one?"

"Oh, shut up," she said, and gave him a light punch on the arm. He'd already made her day and there was nothing he could say that would spoil it.

In fact, she would even dare to say that nothing could happen that day that could dampen her mood. Asia rolled away and hopped onto her feet. "Come on. Time to go explore the island."

"Yes, boss," Rico said in a teasing tone then got up to stand by her. "I'll be your tour guide," he said, with a flourish. "And now, if you'll just follow me." They set off along the beach toward a tiny river that flowed into the sea. As they strolled along Rico pointed out various trees that lined the sand and told her their names. He was even able to identify many of the shrubs along the seacoast. Asia listened intently, surprised at his knowledge of the flora of the island.

They got to the river and Asia realized that it was really no more than a stream. They took off their sandals and waded barefoot through the water which was almost ice-cold.

"It's bubbling from an underground spring," Rico told her, "and that's why it's so cool."

After crossing the stream, they walked along the beach another twenty minutes or so, then they turned onto a grassy path that led inland. "What if we get lost?" Asia asked, as she stared at the mass of trees in the interior. "Do you know the island that well?"

"Crossed it at least a hundred times," he said. "You're safe with me, Asia. Didn't I tell you you're in good hands?"

"Uh, huh," she said, still staring ahead, and still not convinced they were totally safe. What if there were wild animals Rico hadn't encountered before? What if they ran into quicksand? "Maybe we should go back now," she said. "In fact," she continued, and pointed to the sky, "it's sort of gray right now. Maybe it's going to rain?"

"Nonsense. I checked the weather report before we headed out this morning. Sunny skies all day."

"Well, it's not sunny now," she pointed out and made to turn back.

"So, after all that big talk about being in charge," he scoffed, "Asia Miller is nothing but a chicken."

"What did you say?" Asia turned on him.

"Chicken," he said again, and the laughter tumbled from his lips.

"We'll see about that," she said, and headed up the path ahead of him. She'd shown him the other side of her, so now he wasn't expecting a wilting flower. She was supposed to be bold and fearless. So, she would be. She would go a little way in; not too far, just enough to show him she was no wimp.

Rico followed and soon overtook her on the path. He ended up leading the way, totally messing up her plan to lead them a short distance and then turn back. With him leading, there was no telling how far inland he'd go.

"I want to show you something," he said over his shoulder. "A waterfall with a pool at the bottom. We can take a dip."

"Sounds...lovely," she said, all the while thinking, 'maybe we should go back now'.

They'd walked ten more minutes up the path when Asia heard the first rumble of thunder. She stopped and looked up, but it was like being in a tropical rainforest. The foliage was so thick overhead that they could only see patches of the sky. And it was gray. Not teh light gray it had been when they turned onto the path but a deep and ominous gray.

"Uh, oh," Rico said, looking up, too. "Looks like rain."

Asia could have slapped him. Wasn't that what she'd been saying all this time?

"Let's go back," she said, already turning around.

And then a streak of lightning ripped across the sky. Asia jumped, almost knocking Rico over for the second time that day.

"It's okay," he said. "No need to be scared." He put out a hand to steady her.

"I'm not scared," she muttered, and clung to his hand.

The two of them started running back the way they'd come but they knew it was hopeless. With all the walking they'd done, it would take them over half an hour to get back to the boat.

Then, it started to rain. Huge drops fell from the sky, the kind you saw only on a tropical island. It came swift and sudden, the only thing saving them being the thick canopy of leaves overhead.

By the time they broke out of the trees and reached the beach, the rain was coming down in torrents. Thunder rolled and lightning streaked over the water. For Rico and Asia, there was no more need to hide from the rain. They were both soaked straight through. That was the least of their problems. With the lightning flashing they were both in danger of getting struck.

"Shouldn't we stay under the trees?" Asia yelled as they raced across the sand.

"No," Rico yelled back. "Lightning and trees. No good."

In addition to the rain, the wind was whipping into them, making it all the more difficult to be heard.

"Best bet," he yelled, "reach the boat."

The boat? Asia wasn't too sure about that. The sea, tranquil as glass just hours before, was a rolling, roaring mass that reflected the gray of the sky. It was scary to look at, with its waves rising high and crashing into the shore. How could the weather have changed so fast?

No time to think now. She ran with all her might, struggling to keep up with Rico, but each time she fell behind, he stopped to wait, then grabbed her hand, then off they went again.

They were almost at the stream but it, like the rest of nature, had turned into a monster. Water rushed from the interior and down toward the sea, making the river three times its original size.

"*Carajo!*" Rico swore as they stood staring at the swirling water. Then, he moved. Clutching her hand, he ran upstream along the grassy bank. "There's a narrow section up here," he yelled. "I've seen it before. If it hasn't widened, we can cross there."

Rico was right. Higher upstream the water flow was much narrower than below. Still, it must have widened there, too, because it certainly was not of a width where you could easily step across.

"We'll have to jump," Rico yelled.

Asia's eyes widened. Easy for him to say. His legs were twice the length of hers.

He must have seen her hesitation. "It's our only chance of getting back to the boat." He squeezed her hand. "Come on, Asia. We can do it."

As the rain pelted them, she stared up into his face and he looked so determined that she felt she had to try.

She nodded. "Okay, let's do it."

Quickly, they devised a plan. They walked several yards away from the stream to give themselves enough of a running start. Then Rico looked down at her. "I won't let you go, Asia. Just trust me."

She sucked in her breath then nodded.

"Ready?" he yelled.

"Ready."

And they took off running at full speed, Rico still holding her hand in a tight grip. They raced toward the stream and, without stopping, they leaped across, the momentum of the run carrying them to the other side. The power in Rico's hand pulled Asia farther than she could ever have gone on her own. They landed - deep in mud - on the other side.

"We did it," she screeched.

But if was as if Rico didn't hear her. He pulled her up and out of the mud then took off running again, dragging her behind.

Within minutes, they were close enough to see the boat bobbing and rolling in the savage wind and crashing waves, banging into the sturdy plank of the dock.

Only then, did Rico release her hand. "The rope is too loose," he yelled. "I've got to secure the boat."

"But why?" Asia looked at the angry ocean then at Rico. "It's dangerous."

"If I don't, we won't have a boat. We need it to get back."

Before she could say another word in protest, he turned and ran toward the dock, leaving her standing in the rain.

Stupid, stupid man. She didn't care about any damned boat. She was afraid for him. What if he got hurt? God, why did men have to be such daredevils?

She ran after him, but he was already at the end of the dock, struggling with the rope he'd used to secure the boat. Maybe she could help.

She raced down the dock toward him. He would never be able to pull the boat in all by himself. "I'm coming," she yelled. She was almost upon him when, to her horror, she saw the boat lurch and, as if in slow motion, Rico pitched forward and over the edge.

CHAPTER SEVEN

"Rico!" Asia screamed. Jesus Christ, Rico was gone. She ran the remaining yards to the edge and dropped to her knees. God, please don't let him be dead.

Then she saw him. Rico was in the water, still clinging to the rope he was trying to secure, and he was alive.

But he was in danger. The boat could swing back and smash against the dock, crushing Rico in the process.

"Rico," she shrieked, "let go and take my hand. You have to get out."

He looked up at her and she could see the strain on his face. Of course, he knew the danger he was in. He was struggling to get out. But it was no easy task to climb onto the dock when the swirling water was doing its best to suck him down and under.

Asia was bending over, reaching her hand down to him, when he yelled, "Move away. You'll fall over."

She backed away a little, but not far. She had to help him.

And then she saw it. A rope hanging off the other end of the dock. *Dear God, please let it be long enough*. She dashed over and grabbed it then dragged it up, the entire length of it, and ran back to the other side. To her relief it was just long enough to hand down to where Rico could reach it.

"Pull yourself up with this," she shouted. "Quick." She was watching the boat and it was bobbing dangerously close to Rico's head.

He looked up, hair plastered down on his head and almost covering his eyes. When he saw the lifeline, he grabbed it and tugged, then in one swift move he let go of the boat mooring and grabbed this new line with both hands. He pulled up, his muscles straining as he fought the sucking water. Then, he was climbing up and out of the water, until finally he collapsed onto the deck.

"Rico." Asia reached for him. "Thank God."

Now, he was moving again, pushing himself up with his arms. "Asia," he said, still panting from his efforts, "we have to get off the dock. Not safe."

She nodded and bent down to help him to his feet, then she threw his arm over her shoulder and supported him as they hurried back to the shore.

She looked around. Where could they go? There was nowhere to shelter, nowhere to hide.

"The lightning," Rico said, his voice still breathless. "Stay away from the tall trees. Try to find...low bushes where we can shelter."

She did as he said and led him to a copse of thick bushes that were not too close to the trees. There. they sheltered from the whipping wind and stinging rain, clinging to each other for what little warmth they could find.

Asia didn't know how long the storm lasted. It could have been one hour; it could have been four. She'd lost all sense of time. But when the winds finally died down and the rain ceased, she was exhausted.

She looked down at Rico and his head was still resting on her chest, his eyes closed, his arms wrapped around her. She frowned. He couldn't be asleep, could he? In all this?

"Rico," she whispered. "It's gone."

"Hmm," he groaned.

"The storm. It's gone," she said, more firmly. "We have to go check on the boat."

"Oh," he said, then stifled a yawn.

"Were you sleeping?" she asked. "You were, weren't you? Typical man. Guys can sleep through anything."

She pushed him off her chest, denying him any further use of her body as a headrest.

He put up his hands and rubbed his eyes, looking for all the world like a child waking from slumber. Then, as she stood, he blinked up at her like an owl.

"Come on, Rico," she said, annoyed at his slouchy behavior. "We have to go check on the boat. You're acting all cozy and comfortable, like you're in your bedroom. We're on a deserted island, remember?"

Rico blinked again, then he squinted up at her.

That made her even angrier. The man hadn't moved an inch. "You know what, I'll go check on the boat myself." She turned and marched away. She wasn't going to wait on a man who didn't seem to understand the seriousness of their situation.

"Asia?"

She heard Rico call her name, but she kept on walking. "Asia, please. I need you. I...can't see."

What the hell? That stopped her in her tracks. Had something happened to Rico in the water? Had he suddenly gone blind?

She turned and ran back to where she'd left him by the bushes. She dropped to her knees and stared into his face. "Rico? Are you all right?"

He blinked then squinted, the effort making his brows furrow. Then, he smiled. "I can see you now. I'm okay."

That floored her. Didn't he just say he couldn't see? "What kind of game are you playing?" she demanded. "First, you can't see, then you can see. Which is it?"

He raised his eyebrows and gave a boyish pout. "Both, I'm afraid. I'm severely myopic. Can't see a thing past my nose."

"But you don't even wear glasses."

"Yes, I do. But only at home." He shrugged. "I wear contact lenses the rest of the time."

Now, Asia understood. "You lost your contacts in the water."

Rico nodded, then he dropped his eyes and dug his fingers into the sand. He crushed the sand in his hand and did not look up again.

Asia dropped to the ground and sat beside him. Just before he dropped his eyes, she'd seen a look flash across his face, a look that told her he felt helpless, and he hated it. He was probably so used to being in control that he had no idea how to handle being dependent on someone else.

She stared out at the ocean, bluish gray but surprisingly calm, then she said, "Have you ever thought of laser correction?"

He shook his head. "I don't want anyone shooting lasers into my eyes. What if they make me go blind?"

"Rico, I can't believe you think that way. This is the twenty-first century. Hundreds of people have that surgery done every day."

"Surgery," he repeated. "Not on *my* eyes. Never."

She shook her head in exasperation. "You are so old school. Everybody is doing it."

"Let them. I won't." His tone was obstinate.

Asia sighed, but she didn't say another word on the subject. She could tell that no amount of arguing would make him change his mind. She wouldn't even waste her time.

She got up and tried to brush the sand from her bottom. Not an easy task when the sand was stuck to damp clothing. "Well, you stay here while I go check on the boat."

"I'm coming with you," he said, and pushed up from the ground to stand beside her.

"But you can't see a thing," she objected.

"And that's why I'm not letting you leave me here. Anywhere you go, I go. And besides, I've got to stay close to you," he said. "Make sure you don't do anything stupid."

"Look who's talking," she scoffed. "The man who traveled miles out to sea with one pair of contact lenses and no spare."

That shut him up fast. Asia saw his lips tighten and the expression on his face told her he was pissed. She didn't care. He was used to reprimanding his workers. Let him get a taste of his own medicine for a change.

Before she could move, Rico set off by himself, his head down, eyes squinting at the ground right in front of his toes. He moved steadily but slowly, obviously unable to see much farther ahead. She could guess what he was going through. Everything ahead must be one blurry mass. He probably couldn't even see the boat in the distance. But she'd wounded his pride, and that pride would not make him stop and wait for her help.

Well, let him go. If he wanted to march off blindly and fall into a hole, then that was his problem.

The thought had hardly registered in her mind when she saw Rico stumble. Her heart lurched, but he righted himself and kept on going.

Enough was enough. She ran to him and grabbed his arm. He shook her off.

"Will you stop?" She grabbed his arm again. "You're acting like a child. Now, hold my hand."

It was a good thing Rico couldn't see his own face. His mouth was set in a mutinous pout that made her want to smile, but she kept her face serious. Asia slipped her hand in his and began to walk beside him. She guided him around a patch of sharp rocks and onto the smoother sections ,and so they walked until they were finally back at the dock.

"Is the boat all right?" Rico asked, as he stared ahead.

She was sure he could see the boat, or at least the big white form of it, but he probably couldn't see any finer details. She let go of his hand. "I'll go check."

"Wait. I don't want you going in. It might be dangerous." He squinted hard then shook his head in obvious frustration. "Just stay on the dock and look. You have to be careful."

She walked to the end and peered at the boat as it now bobbed gently in the water that looked peaceful and innocent as if it hadn't been battering that same boat against the planks just hours before.

"So far, so good," she said. "I haven't seen any damage."

He nodded, obviously pleased with the news.

"I'm going on board, okay. I want to see if the engine still works."

He frowned at that. "What did I tell you, Asia?'

"But Rico, how will we know that the boat is really all right? We can't just stand here all day watching it." She folded her arms across her chest. "Let's just be sensible about this. I'm going on board."

As she watched his face, it went from adamant to frustrated to resigned. "All right," he said grudgingly, "but be careful."

She didn't wait for him to change his mind. Carefully holding on to the edge, she climbed into the boat, her sandaled feet sloshing in the water that had gathered at the bottom. She only hoped the boat hadn't sprung a leak. She checked around for damages or holes but could find none. All that water in the boat had probably sloshed over the side in the storm.

Now, to check the engine. She looked up at Rico. "Do you have the key?"

He dug into his pocket and stretched out his hand to her.

She inserted the key and when she turned the engine it kicked in immediately. "Yes," she cheered, and grinned up at him. "Problem solved."

She could see the relief wash over his face. But then, his face clouded over and he shook his head. "Not quite. I can't see, remember?"

"I can. All you have to do is give me the instructions and I'll get us home."

He shook his head. "I don't think so. It's better if we stay put. My people will know where I am. They'll come."

Then a thought came to her. "Hey, where's your cell phone?"

He patted the pockets of his jeans. "Gone. Lost in the water. It wouldn't have worked from here, anyway. No cell towers. Try the boat radio."

She tried it, turning knobs, shouting into it, listening. She shook her head. "Nothing but static."

"It must be the storm. Come on out, then. Let's just go back up the beach and wait."

"Hey, don't we even vote on it? Why do you automatically assume we do things your way?"

"Because I'm the man and I'm responsible for your safety."

"That's so chauvinistic."

"That may be," he said, "but we're safer on land rather than floating around in the ocean with a navigator who can't even read the instruments."

Asia admitted defeat then. She certainly did not want to be lost out in the middle of the big blue sea. "Well, monsieur," she said, with a wry grin, "I guess you're stuck with my company for a few more hours." He was smiling at her, so she guessed he didn't mind.

She hopped out of the boat and back on to the deck, then took Rico's hand. Together, they walked back to shore, where Rico plopped down on a sandy bank while Asia went off, but not too far away, to see if she could find where their blanket and picnic basket had gone.

Within a couple of hours of their setting up camp - lying on the damp blanket that Asia found, and eating the rest of the food that, happily, had survived the storm - they heard the roar of a motorboat in the distance. As Rico had predicted, his personal staff had arranged a search party as soon as the storm lifted.

As the second motorboat shot forward, then came close and pulled alongside them, Asia's heart slid off its precarious perch and slid down to settle in its rightful place behind her ribs.

She heard the cheers and whoops before the saw the men. "Hey, boss! You okay?"

"Okay, now that you guys are here for me." He turned to look at Asia. "For us."

Rico wasted no time in directing Asia toward the rescue boat and carefully handing her over to the burly man stretching out his hand. Soon, she was up and out of the first boat and then, after being guided onto the second, safely ensconced in its cabin, with Rico close behind.

As they set off, Asia peered out the window to look back on the island, so peaceful and then so passionate, and in her heart was a twinge of sadness. It was here that she'd found a new connection with Rico.

She'd shown him another side of her, and she'd seen him at his most vulnerable. And then they'd lain down after the storm, side by side on the blanket, just talking about their families, their lives, and a whole lot more. Now, it was time to go.

But would things change, would the balance be lost, when they got back to their own world?

CHAPTER EIGHT

Something about him had changed. Rico couldn't quite say what, but he just felt different. He didn't take life quite so seriously these days, and he'd actually caught himself singing in the shower. Twice this week!

Another week had passed before he knew it and, unlike his weekends of the previous few months, he was looking forward to this one. And the reason for his anticipation was no mystery. He was going to see Asia tomorrow.

Although he'd been embarrassed as hell when he'd lost his contact lenses on the island, things had turned out rather well in the end. After the storm he and Asia had relaxed on the beach, just talking, and for him it had been a rare and special experience. He couldn't recall doing that with anyone before. His life had always been focused and driven. When had he had the time to just lie back, let the island breeze flow over him, and share his thoughts with a beautiful woman? And what a woman she was. She seemed to understand him so well. It was as if she could read into his soul.

He'd been anxious to call her during the week, just to talk to her some more, but each time he would have called, she'd seemed distracted or busy. He began to wonder if he'd done something to offend her. But, as was his nature, he'd persisted until finally he'd gotten her to agree to see him again.

Rico frowned as he stared out the window at his office. Something about him had changed all right. He, Enrico Xavier Megalos, had just spent the better part of an afternoon daydreaming about a woman. God help him.

· · ❧ · ·

TONIGHT WAS THE FIRST time Rico had asked Asia out and not ordered her to wear jeans. It felt good to slip into her well-loved 'little black dress' and slide her feet into high-heeled sandals. For this date, she would look and feel like a real woman.

She touched a little perfume to her pulse points, the final touch to her preparations, then sat back and stared at herself in the mirror. He'd told her he liked her hair down, so she'd let it fall around her shoulders. She smiled, liking the look. Asia, the tigress, was back.

She chuckled to herself and got up. It was a minute to seven and she knew his car would pull up right on time. She picked up her purse and walked to the door just as a sleek black Lincoln town car pulled up to the curb.

Heart pounding in anticipation, she walked up to the car just as the chauffeur, the same one she'd met that first night, came around to hold the door open. She thanked him, then peered in, and was surprised to find it empty. She looked back at the chauffeur. "Where is Mr. Megalos?"

"Mr. Megalos had some final preparations to make," he said mysteriously. "He asked that I take you to him as soon as possible."

"Oh," she said, still confused, but she slid into the seat, and he closed the door.

Asia had other questions, like where, exactly, was Rico? And what preparations was he making? But she had a feeling the driver was instructed to keep things secret, so she didn't even waste her time asking. With a sigh she settled back into the seat to enjoy the ride.

It didn't take long for Asia to realize that they were on the way to Fisher Island, the wealthiest neighborhood in Miami-Dade county, and also one of the wealthiest in the entire country. The ferry took the car across, and into that exclusive community, then they set off. She guessed that Rico was already at a restaurant, waiting for her.

But when the car turned through the gates of what could only be described as an island estate, she knew that this was no restaurant, but Rico's home. They drove up to a grand mansion of white and gold set in the middle of rolling green lawns and the ocean in the background.

As soon as the car pulled up in front, wide double doors opened, and a uniformed butler came down the stairs to greet her.

"Welcome, Miss Miller," he said with a bow, his British accent crisp and polished.

The,n he escorted her up the steps and into what looked like a grand ballroom. "I will take you to Mr. Megalos directly," he said, and led the way down a wide marble-tiled hallway along which stood sculptures that looked like they were straight from the temple of Parthenon on top of the Acropolis.

At the end of the hallway the butler turned right, and Asia found herself in an elegant dining room graced with a candle-lit table set for two. And there, looking for all the world like the hero on the cover of a romance novel - tall, dark and extremely handsome - was Rico. Dressed in white shirt open at the collar, and black pants, he could have been the gorgeous swash-buckling pirate that maidens loved to swoon over.

"Welcome to my home," he said, and stepped forward to take Asia by the hand and pull her into the room.

"Rico, what a...surprise. I thought I'd be meeting you at a restaurant."

"That was the original plan," he admitted, "but at the last minute, I changed my mind. I decided I wanted to make you dinner myself."

"You?" She stared at him, incredulous. "Can you cook?"

He gave her a wounded look. "Is the lady questioning my abilities?" "No," she said, with a quick laugh. "Not at all. I look forward to enjoying a meal made by your hands."

And enjoy it, she did. Roasted chicken flavored with red wine, baby carrots steamed with tiny potatoes in a garlic sauce, and a vegetable potpie with a crust that melted in her mouth.

"You did all this?" she asked.

"Well, I did have some help," he said, with an almost guilty smile, "from my chef."

"I knew it," she teased.

"But, no," he said, putting his hands up, as if to profess his innocence, "I really did most of the work. He was just there to guide me from time to time."

"Well, however you did it, I'm impressed. I really enjoyed it."

After dinner, they moved to a private sitting room, where Rico left her for a moment. "Dry eyes," he explained. "Need some eye drops."

When he came back, he was wearing glasses.

"So, that's what you look like in glasses," she teased. "Mr. Four Eyes."

"Who're you calling Four Eyes," he growled, and reached for her, then dragged her into his arms. "I should punish you for that."

"I didn't do anything," she said, giving him a look of innocence.

"Shall I list your sins?" he asked, as he smiled down at her. "First, you avoided me all week."

"I did not," she protested.

"You know you did," he said, his voice adamant. "Every time I called, you were rushing off somewhere. I know that trick."

She bit her lip, feeling guilty. "I'm sorry," she said. "You're right. I was avoiding you, but only because I thought you needed some space, in case you had regrets...about us."

"You crazy woman," he chided. "What the heck are you talking about? I have none. Do you?"

She shook her head.

"And are you ready for sin number two?"

"I have a second sin?"

"Yes. You called me Four Eyes. Now, come take your punishment like a man."

She began to giggle at his lame joke, but he put an end to that when his mouth swooped down, and he captured hers in a kiss that made her toes curl. When he finally released her, she was gasping.

By this time, Asia was a mass of tingling nerves. Every inch of her was aware of Rico - the feel of his lips against hers, the solid breadth of his chest as it crushed her breasts, his masculine hardness as it pressed into her. She wanted more of him, so much more. But was she treading in dangerous waters?

She had to break the tension. Without warning, she reached up and slipped Rico's glasses off his nose. Before he could react, she pulled out of his arms and skipped away.

"Hey, why'd you do that?" He blinked, then squinted, trying hard to see her. "Come back here, you little devil."

"Never," she chortled, and went to stoop beside an armchair in the corner. So, she was being immature, acting like a bratty kid. So what? It was fun, having the upper hand on Rico.

"Are you trying to add to your list of sins?" He put out his hands and began to creep around the room, trying to find her. "Once I have you, you will be punished. Best to give up now, before it's too late."

She only giggled some more. She realized that was a stupid thing to do, when he turned and headed in her direction. Right then, everything was a blur to him, but there was nothing wrong with his hearing.

She dashed away just in time, and laughed when he bumped into the standing lamp. Luckily, it didn't topple over. She decided to put an end to the teasing. This cat and mouse game was fun, but it was ratcheting up the sexual tension that had been building inside her. She'd thought the game would take her mind away from her desire for Rico, but instead, the hunt, playful though it was, had only made her want him more.

"Rico," she called out from the other end of the room, "let's make a deal. I'll give you your glasses back if you agree to do everything I say."

"Everything?" he asked, with a lascivious smile.

"Everything," she replied, her tone breathless.

"Deal." He held out his hands, palms upward. "I am yours, mademoiselle. Do with me, what you will."

Gosh, that sounded good. Her mouth went dry in anticipation. He was offering himself to her and she planned on taking full advantage. She straightened her back, and with a sniff, she walked over and took his outstretched hands. She'd hooked the glasses onto the front of her dress. She wasn't giving them back; not just yet. She was enjoying keeping him slightly off balance.

"Take me to your bedroom," she said boldly. "I have an assignment for you. Let's see how well you can execute." She released his hands and reached up to pull his head down. "If you do a good job," she whispered in his ear, "I might just give you your glasses back."

She heard the laughter rumble deep in his chest, but he did not say a word. He simply nodded and, taking her hand, he turned to leave the sitting room.

Rico had no problem finding his bedroom without the help of his glasses. He led her down the hall, and within seconds, he was pushing open the door to a massive bedroom with a king-sized bed in the middle.

Asia pulled her hand from Rico's grasp and pushed the door shut behind them. Then, she sauntered over to the bed and sat down. "Come to me," she whispered, and held out her arms. She was warming to the game, getting into her role as seductress. She'd set out to tame this man, and she planned to do it in more ways than one.

When he came to sit beside her, Asia ran her fingers through his hair, then stood up so that she was the one looking down at him. Then, she lowered her lips to his forehead, his cheeks, the tip of his nose, giving him heated little kisses that were just a hint of her passion for him.

He lifted his mouth, searching for her with his lips, but she refused him that pleasure. She would not give him what he wanted, not yet.

With trembling fingers, she began to undo the buttons on his shirt. Then, she slid the garment off his shoulders and stepped back to admire the beauty of his lean, muscled torso as it gleamed in the pale moonlight that stole through the window.

He reached out a hand to touch her, but she held his wrist. "No," she whispered. "Unzip me first." She slipped the glasses off the front of her dress where she'd hooked it, and laid it on the night table, then she turned her back to him. As the zipper went down, she slid the straps from her shoulders and let her dress fall to the floor. Then, she turned to him, dressed only in bra and panties, and her heart soared as she saw desire flare in his dark eyes.

"Lie back on the pillows," she commanded, and couldn't help but smile when he moved willingly, eagerly, to fulfill her order. When it came to fulfilling his desire, a man could be as obedient as a lamb.

Asia climbed onto the bed, deciding to be even more daring than ever. She straddled Rico, her knees pressed into the bed on either side of him, then she pushed his arms up, grabbed his wrists and pressed them into the pillows, trapping them on either side of his head.

"Are you going to give me everything I want?" she growled playfully.

"*Oui, mademoiselle.*" His voice was raspy, as if he was having trouble breathing.

"And you will follow my every command?"

"*Oui, mademoiselle,*" he repeated.

"Then, kiss me here." She thrust forward, her lace-covered breasts just inches from his lips, her arousal evident in the sharp points of her nipples.

Obediently, he lifted his head to plant a warm kiss on the exposed fullness of one breast then the other. Then, he captured a laced-covered nipple between his teeth, and tugged and nibbled before moving to the other nipple. When she gasped in delight, he gripped the right bra cup with his teeth, and pulled it down and immediately slipped the tortured nipple into his mouth, where he sucked and soothed until Asia felt she would swoon from the pleasure.

He moved to the other, where he exposed the nipple and administered the same tantalizing caress, and Asia's bones melted like chocolate in the rays of the sun. She sagged into him, breathing hard. Before she could recover, Rico pulled his wrist from her grasp and wrapped his arms around her. Then, he rolled over, trapping her beneath him.

"What else does *mademoiselle* want?" he whispered, his lips so close that his breath tickled her ear. "I promised to give you everything."

"I want...you." Asia was panting now.

He bent his head and kissed her on the lips. "Whatever the lady desires." Rico slid off the bed and loosened his belt. Soon, belt, trousers and boxer shorts were sliding down his lean legs to the floor. He stood straight and tall, his erection proudly declaring his state of arousal.

Inexplicably, Asia felt a blush creep up and over her body. How could she be embarrassed when she was the one who had started all this? As he reached for his wallet on the nightstand, she closed her eyes. As soon as he was sheathed, he would be all hers, and she was both eager and afraid at the thought.

When Rico climbed back onto the bed and reached for her, Asia did not open her eyes. Before, she'd come off as bad, bold and sure of herself. Now, not so much. What if after tonight, Rico never wanted to see her again? There were men like that - when they got you in bed, once they'd got a taste of the forbidden fruit, they lost all interest. What if that happened to her?

She was turning her face away, the thought filling her mind, when Rico said, his voice so gentle and soothing that her heart melted, "It's okay, Asia. I won't hurt you. Just relax."

Then, he loosened the clasp on her bra, and moved to slide her panties down her legs. Softly, he slid heated palms up her legs, until his hands rested on her hips.

Her eyes still tightly closed, Asia felt his hand slide over her mound. She stiffened, but the gentle fingers moved down to stroke the sensitive bud between her legs, making her bones liquefy, making her moan. Under Rico's expert caress, the tension in her legs eased, and she shifted to give him greater access. He stroked and caressed, his hands the source of such sweetness that she almost cried out in pleasure.

To her relief, after sheathing himself, Rico moved up her body and positioned himself over her. "It will be fine, Asia," he whispered. "You're ready for me now. I won't hurt you."

And then, he sank deep inside her, driving his manhood into her core.

Asia cried out, her body filled with the hardness of him, and as he thrust into her, she lifted her legs to wrap them around him. And then, she clung to him, meeting his every thrust, taking all that he could give.

And then, she was climbing, climbing to that highest peak of rapture, her breath coming fast, her body tingling all over.

And then, she was over the edge, falling, falling into a sea of sensation that had her trembling all over.

Rico must have felt her reach her climax, because as hot lava exploded inside her, he gave a guttural groan and plunged deep inside, where he stayed, his hips jerking, his body releasing all its pent-up passion.

They lay there, wrapped in each other's arms, and for a long time they did not move.

And as Asia lay cradled in Rico's arms a wave of sadness washed over her. She bit her lip, almost on the verge of tears.

Stupid woman that she was, she'd gone and fallen in love with Enrico Megalos, a man who could have any woman in the world, a man who would probably never settle for someone like her.

CHAPTER NINE

Asia drew into her shell, totally avoiding any contact with Rico. She needed time to be alone, time to think.

Coming to grips with the fact that she was in love with one of the most desired bachelors in Florida - and one of the least likely to settle down - was a very difficult task. So what, if she'd been working with him for over a month? So what, if they'd been seeing each other after that, and had mind-blowing sex? It was time for her to face reality. She had to stop living in dreamland and pull out of this pretend relationship because she knew how it would end - she was the one who was going to get hurt.

She planned an impromptu visit to her parents, happy to tell Rico that she would be in Canada for the next two weeks. At least, she had a good reason for not keeping in touch. By the time she returned to Florida, she would have built up enough strength to have a talk with him, let him know it was best that they didn't see each other anymore. That was, assuming that he would even remember her after she'd been gone for that length of time. Men could be fickle creatures.

But when Asia got back home two weeks later, there was a message on her answering machine that threw all her well-made plans upside down.

"I miss you, Asia. Call me as soon as you get back."

Now, what was a girl to do? She loved him. She'd finally given up fighting that sad fact. But could she risk her heart? Did he really miss her or was it just the sex?

She heaved a sigh and flopped down onto the sofa, more confused now than when she'd left for Canada. She wanted to see him. Desperately. But she knew that if they found themselves alone, she would be the one ripping his clothes off, not the other way around.

And then, where would that leave her? The stupidest thing a girl could do was to let a man know how much she wanted him. Unless he'd already made a commitment. And Rico hadn't.

She sat there nibbling her fingernail, and then a thought came to her - maybe she could see Rico, but on neutral ground. And she would get a chance to observe him in a totally different environment, get to see who he really was. She would invite him to the youth center.

. . ⚜ . .

IT WASN'T UNTIL THE following weekend that Rico was able to find an afternoon free to visit the youth center. When she'd called and invited him, he'd been intrigued, and had willingly accepted, but then he'd followed immediately by telling her he wanted her to come over and he would be sending a car for her. She refused. She didn't say as much to him, but she was determined not to fall under his spell and into bed with him again, not until she'd figured out how he truly felt about her.

Instead of accepting his invitation, she'd changed the subject. She again went back to what was near and dear to her heart – the youth center. "We got some new equipment at the youth center. I had to use all my contacts, but it worked. We now have everything we need for the basketball court and the gym." At the memory of the thrilled reaction of the boys, Asia couldn't help but smile to herself.

"You really love helping those kids." There was no question in Rico's voice.

"You got that right," she said. "Helping people is my Heaven. What greater joy can there be, than the sweet satisfaction of helping those in need?"

"What greater joy, indeed..." Rico's voice trailed off, as if deep in thought.

"It was a book I read that inspired me," she continued. "It made me realize the importance of, not just wanting to help others, but actually doing something about it."

"Must have been some book."

"Yeah, it was. I got it when I was having one of my 'down' days. I needed a 'perk-me-up', so I bought it – 'How to be Happy', by J. A. Powell. To this day, I don't know if the writer is a man or a woman. All I know is, it's a disabled person who says that, right now, while being disabled, they've never been happier. Found the secret to happiness, they said. Can you guess what it is?"

"What?"

She laughed. "I said, guess."

He was silent for some seconds, like he was thinking. "I know it's not money."

"You got that right."

"So...it must be...friends. Having good friends."

"I'm not going to tell you. Go read it yourself." She chuckled, enjoying how she was screwing with his curiosity. "The secret elixir. Such a simple solution for depression."

"Asia...do you get depressed sometimes?" He sounded concerned.

"Not anymore, I don't. I've got the secret weapon, remember?" Then, before he decided to delve any deeper, she changed the subject. "You're coming by later, right?"

"You got it. I'll be there by four."

It was that reassurance that, later, made Asia keep glancing at the entrance, anxious to see Rico appear.

"So, where's this young man of yours?" Shelley asked for the umpteenth time.

"He's coming," Asia said, trying to keep the exasperation out of her tone. He'd told her he would be there at four o'clock. It was fifteen minutes after. He'd probably gotten stuck in Saturday afternoon traffic.

Or maybe he'd stood her up? He was a billionaire, after all. Too big to mingle with the little people. By eighteen minutes after the hour, she was convinced that her theory was right. And it didn't help that Shelley kept pestering her about when he would arrive.

And then, he ran into the auditorium, a basketball under his arm, wearing T-shirt, sweatpants and sneakers. "Sorry I'm late," he said with a grin, and loped over to give her a peck on the cheek. "I realize I wasn't fully equipped and stopped to get some gear." He pointed to his gym wear. "You like?"

Her heart melting with relief, she smiled back at him. "I like," she said, "Very much." Then, she felt a nudge, and turned to see Shelley by her side.

"Hey, aren't you going to introduce us?" her friend demanded, none too quietly.

"Of course. Rico, this is my very good friend, Shelley Smith. Shelley, Rico Megalos."

"Very pleased to meet you, Rico," Shelley said, taking his hand. She was practically preening for the man. But who could blame her? Today, he looked hot in every sense of the word.

Asia could not tear her eyes from Rico. It had been three weeks since she'd last seen him, and if her body's response was anything to go by, he was not forgotten. At the sight of him, her nipples had turned to pebbles in her blouse, and her heart began to pick up speed. *Calm down, Asia, he's only a man. No need to hyperventilate.*

"So, what do you want me to do?" he asked, his eyes never once leaving her face.

"Well, I did give you the choice of serving dinner or hanging out with the guys."

"I guess my choice is obvious," he said, with a laugh. "Point me to them."

After Asia got Rico situated on the basketball court with the six or seven youngsters there, she went back to help Shelley with the food.

"When I asked him to help out, he wanted to donate money," she said, as she watched him in the distance. He'd just stolen the ball from a tough-looking kid. She was surprised. Rico wasn't half bad on the basketball court.

"Money always helps," Shelley said, her eyes on Rico, too.

"Yes, but our kids need more than that. And anyway, writing a check is easy. It's taking the time to be with them, that counts."

"Well said, sister." Shelley gave a soft chuckle. "But you know what? Your guy seems to be doing okay on both sides. Look at how he just fit right in with the boys. And he's not cutting them any slack, either. They've got to work to get that ball from him."

She was right. Rico seemed like a natural on the basketball court. With his height and trim figure, he moved swiftly and easily, bobbing and weaving toward the basket. The boys, although younger, had nothing over him when it came to scoring a basket.

"Are you thinking what I'm thinking?" Shelley asked.

"Uh, huh." Asia nodded. "With skills like that, he's bound to be a basketball fan..."

"Which means he probably has connections in the basketball world."

Shelley said, finishing Asia's thought. "Next time he comes to the center, we have to introduce him to Robert."

"If there is a next time." Asia rolled her eyes, mocking Shelley's confidence.

"Oh, there will be," Shelley said, with certainty. "I told you we needed some more male role models around here. I think we've found our first candidate."

That evening, Rico stayed until the center closed at nine o'clock, playing game after game with the boys, eating with them and chilling on the benches, telling them stories about being on a semi-professional team in France. The boys listened, open-mouthed, and when it was time to go, the women had to shoo them out. They were so fascinated with Rico that they hardly even wanted to leave.

"Yup," Shelley said, "he's the one."

After the last boy had gone, Rico strolled over to them, his damp T-shirt clinging to his body. "That was good," he said, with a sigh. "I haven't had such a good workout in ages."

"Glad you had fun," Asia said, trying not to stare. The sight of his nipples and broad chest under the damp T-shirt was bringing back memories. It was turning her on.

They stood there staring at each other as if the two of them were the only people there. That was the way it must have seemed, because Shelley suddenly cleared her throat, causing them both to turn.

"Well," she said, putting her hands on her hips, "I can see where this is going. It's as clear as day. You two are in love." She directed a pointed look at Rico. "So, what are you waiting for? When are you going to pop the question?"

Asia's mouth fell open. If the earth could have opened right at that moment, she would have gladly jumped in. How embarrassing. To have your friend demand a marriage proposal on your behalf? Was there anything more pathetic? And what if he thought she was the one who'd put Shelley up to it?

But that wasn't the worst part. No, the absolute worst part was the look on Rico's face. The only word Asia could think of was 'stricken'. The man's face flushed, and he looked so guilty that Asia knew, without a doubt, that marriage to her was the last thing in the world he would ever want.

He wanted her. She had no doubt about that. But he did not want her for his wife.

CHAPTER TEN

That night, Rico lay in bed, the king-sized bed that now seemed much too big for him alone, and he could not sleep. He kept reliving that question Shelley had asked, and he still could not believe it.

Had he been so obvious? Was it that easy to read that he was in love? When Shelley had blurted out the question, he'd been taken aback by her bluntness, but he'd been even more surprised by her perceptiveness. He, who had always prided himself on being a master of his emotions, had been found out.

And then, he thought of Asia, little Mademoiselle Miller, the first woman to try her hand at dominating him. And she'd done it in her own special way. There was no shouting match, no conflict, but she'd taken control of his mind, his heart, and his life. And, to his surprise, he welcomed it.

And he remembered something one of his 'brothers' had said to him, something that now drove home the fact that sometimes you might just have to act on impulse. "Sometimes, if you feel something in your gut, you just gotta act on it," were Storm's words. "Trust your instinct sometimes. Who knows if you'll get a second chance?"

And that was how Rico knew. He had to talk to Asia. He looked at the clock on the wall. Eleven-fourteen. Too late to call. It would have to wait till morning.

ASIA SAT CLENCHING and unclenching her fists as she waited for Rico's car to arrive. This was it; he moment she'd been dreading but had expected all along. Rico had called her early that morning to tell her he needed to see her. She'd suggested they meet next week, but he'd said it couldn't wait. He had to see her this evening.

And this was all taking place the day after Shelley had dropped her bombshell. He'd probably decided it was best to end it before things got out of hand.

So, here she was, waiting for the axe to fall. But she had a plan. She wasn't going to just sit and wait for him to ditch her. She'd known this love affair wasn't going to last and she would tell him so. That way, she wouldn't have to go through the torture of watching him try to wheedle himself out of the situation.

Resolved in her plan, when the car pulled up at her house, she was ready.

Rico looked serious this evening. He'd given her a brief hello, and as soon as she got in, they set off. She was surprised when he pulled off the main road and drove to a deserted corner of the seashore. Then, he turned to her.

"Let's go for a walk," he said. "We need to talk."

They walked along the sand, not speaking, until they came to a sand bank on top of which a thick mat of grass had grown. That was where he invited her to sit and then he sat beside her.

"There's something I should have said to you some time ago," he began, as he stared out at the ocean, "but I've been too stubborn to share my true feelings."

Asia didn't want to hear any more. "It's okay, Rico. I know. You don't have to say another word."

He looked at her and frowned. "You do?"

Asia felt a dark and heavy fog rising up to surround her heart. She was hurting, but she could not let him know. She drew in a shaking breath, then she nodded. "Yes, and I feel the same way. We've had a great time, but I think it's best if we end this now."

"What? Why?" Rico looked at her with eyes full of disbelief. "But I was just about to tell you about my plan."

Why did the man insist on rubbing it in? "You don't need to dump me, Rico," she said, exasperated by his persistence. "I'm going to walk away. You have nothing to worry about."

"But you can't. I was just about to tell you. I'm going to do laser surgery. On my eyes."

Now, it was Asia's turn to look at him in disbelief. "You drag me all the way out here to tell me you're going to do laser surgery on your eyes?" She gave a hiss of frustration. "You could have told me that on the phone."

Rico reached out and took her hand in his. "No, Asia, I couldn't. I wanted to see your face when I told you that you were the one who taught me to take risks. You taught me that I don't have to be on the defensive, and I don't have to be a bully, to be a man."

"And what does that have to do with eye surgery?" She tried pulling her hand away, but he would not let go.

Rico gave her a solemn look. He drew in a deep breath, then let it out in a sigh. "I've never been one to take chances, Asia. I've always been in control. But you taught me..." he frowned, seeming to be struggling to find the right words, "...to give up some of that control and to trust."

He lifted her hand to his lips. Then he kissed it. "I've never trusted anyone with my heart. Until now." He looked away then, and stared out at the waves as they rolled into the shore. "My decision to trust the surgeons is symbolic of an even greater decision I've made." He turned his gaze back to her and this time he was smiling, his look earnest and loving. "Asia, I want to trust my heart to one woman in this world. That woman..." he raised his hand to caress her cheek, "...is you. Asia, my little mademoiselle, will you be my wife?"

Asia's heart lurched in her chest. The air suddenly grew thin, and she felt like she could not breathe. She gasped for air, and then she burst into tears.

"Don't," she cried. "Please don't. You're torturing me."

"*Ma cherie*, what is the matter?" As her body shook with heavy sobs, Rico gathered her into his arms. "Please don't cry."

"Don't play these games with me, Rico," she cried. "It hurts."

"This is not a game, *mon amour*. Not a game. This is for real. I love you."

"Are you...sure?" Her sobs subsided into a hiccup as she stared up at him through tear-filled eyes.

He was smiling down at her, his eyes gentle and kind and true. "I am one hundred percent sure, my love. I am giving my heart to you. Will you take it? Please say yes."

The fog inside Asia dissolved. Rico loved her. At the realization, she felt the light of the sun and all the colors of the rainbow fill her heart. "I will say yes," she whispered, "on one condition."

"What's that?" Rico asked, with a soft smile.

"That you take my heart in exchange for yours. I give you my heart for always. And," she gave him a look of mischief and love, "refusal is not an option."

"Mademoiselle, I accept."

And as the gentle waves rolled in to caress the shore, Asia and Rico, lion tamer and tycoon, celebrated their love with a kiss that joined their hearts...forever.

EPILOGUE

"What did you do to my son?" Carmelita Megalos, looking for all the world like a tiny terrier, was looking up at Asia, arms folded across her buxom bosom, her dark eyes flashing.

Asia sucked in an involuntary breath "N...nothing", she said quickly, her heart tightening in her chest. "He made the decision on his own." She felt the flush rising her face and perspiration prickled her brow. When she'd been invited to meet Rico's parents, she hadn't expected the third degree. The afternoon with them had been going so well, but now it looked like it was taking a turn.

"No," the woman said, shaking her head. "You made him do it."

"I did?"

"You did." The matron's lips curved in smile. "How you did it, I don't know, but I'm so glad you did." Suddenly, she reached out and clasped Asia's hands. "You tamed our wandering wolf. You're the one who finally made him commit. That's why I know you're the perfect partner for *il piccino*. Welcome to the family, my dear."

"Th...thank you." That was all Asia could manage to squeak out, almost sagging in relief as she realized her mistake.

"A moment with the little lady all to ourselves."

At the sound of the booming voice, Asia turned, and suddenly found herself folded into a big bear hug. Within seconds, she was released, and when she looked up, it was into the laughing face of the patriarch of the Megalos family, his eyes twinkling as he smiled at her. "You are *la ragazza* who corralled our *cavallo. Grazie.*"

Asia parted her lips to speak but a laughing yell cut into the conversation. "Hey, you guys. Leave Asia alone."

She looked in the direction of the laughter and saw the love of her life looking so luscious that her heart lurched.

A form-fitting T shirt covering his muscled frame, sunshades shielding his gaze from the sun's glare, Rico loped over to take Asia's hand in his. "Leave her be, you two," he said, with a laugh. "Asia's all mine, now." He took her hand then glanced at his parents. "Let me have a little time with my lady. You've been hogging her all afternoon."

Despite the protests of his parents, Rico directed Asia away from the back patio and she soon found herself strolling along a pathway that led to an alcove adorned with acacias in the corners, and trellises covered in the glossy green leaves of hydrangeas, bougainvilleas and wisterias.

There, her husband-to-be led her over to a cushioned wicker couch. As she sat down on the soft surface, Rico settled beside her.

He was smiling "How are you doing? Feeling overwhelmed yet?"

Asia nodded. "Sort of." Then, she let out a soft sigh and smiled back at him. "But I'm glad you let me meet your family."

He chuckled. "So, what do you think?"

"You have a lovely family. There's no doubt about that. But…" she bit her lip, feeling almost embarrassed to say it. "…it threw me off a bit when you left me by myself."

Rico laughed. "You weren't by yourself. You were with my parents."

Asia grimaced. "That was the scary part."

"They love you. I could see that from a mile away."

"I couldn't. I thought they hated me."

"Why the heck did you think that?"

"Your mom. She kept glaring at me."

Rico laughed. "That's just Mom. Sometimes, she looks like she's mad, even when she's not. It's that bad habit of hers, wrinkling her brows for everything, good and bad. My fault, I think."

"That brought a smile to Asia's lips. "And why would it be your fault?"

"What do you think? Constant troublemaker. And grumpy grouch. That's what they called me."

Asia smiled and stepped forward to wrap her arms around Rico's waist. "Not anymore, you're not."

He smiled and pulled her into his warm embrace. "Guess not. This morning, I had to laugh when she told me her grumpy grouch was gone, and she loved my new mellow mood. Must be all because of you, she said. And she's right." He squeezed her tighter. "All because of you."

She lifted her face from his chest "But I didn't…"

"You did." He tilted his face forward to place a peck on her forehead. "Because of you, new perspective, new me. And no-one loves it more than the HR director." He chuckled. "You did your job, and more."

The words, so simply and sweetly spoken, made Asia's heart melt. It wasn't like she'd done anything sensational. She'd only done the job she'd set out to do.

But this additional asset, this now mellow man, was a precious perk she would cherish for the rest of her days

THE END

Thank you for reading!

'Helping others is my Heaven. What greater joy can there be, than the sweet satisfaction of helping someone in need?'

TO TAME A TYCOON

Sneak Preview of the next in the series:
THE BILLIONAIRE BROTHERHOOD SERIES
VOLUME 6

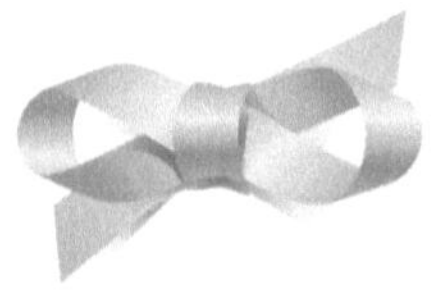

Sweet Seduction
CHAPTER ONE

The gun was pointed at Brent Baker's heart, but he felt no fear. No, what he felt was...anticipation. He was prepared to die.

Jake McKoy sat back in his chair and stared out the window. Where did he go from here? He'd started this story three weeks earlier and still had not gotten past this scene.

Truth be told, he hadn't written anything of sense in the last three years. And he didn't know if he ever would.

With a sigh he threw the pen down and got up from the kitchen table. He had to do something to get the creative juices flowing again. Three years was a long time for a dry spell. His publishers weren't going to wait forever.

He'd set up a writing office in the tiny self-contained studio apartment at the bottom of the garden and equipped it with a desk, a computer, a file cabinet and books. That hadn't worked. He'd abandoned that and tried the good old kitchen table. His progress so far? Twelve sad pages of drivel. He just could not get into the story. Were his writing days over?

In a last ditch attempt he decided to go down to the basement and dig up a book he used to read – *Lighting the Creative Spark*. The book wouldn't tell him anything he didn't already know but maybe, just maybe, it would get him going again.

He'd flipped on the light and was halfway down the stairs when he realized that something was not quite right. There was an unfamiliar sound, a steady tapping against the basement window. He paused on the fourth step then frowned. Who the heck was at his window? He glanced down, looking for some kind of weapon – just in case. His eyes fell on a broom leaning in the corner at the foot of the stairs. It would have to do.

Jake went down the stairs, quietly but swiftly, and grasped the broom handle. Then he peered round the corner.

"What the-"

There wasn't a soul tapping at the glass. The sound he'd heard was water dripping from a pipe above his head, falling into a massive pool of water below.

Just what he needed. A flooded basement to start his Friday.

He peered up into the shadows at the exposed pipe. That alone could not have done this much damage. It was like he had his own personal indoor pond. There had to be something else going on down below.

He rolled his pants up to his knees and waded into the ankle-deep water and as he did he groaned aloud. Even if he got the leak fixed how the heck was he going to get this place dried out and cleaned up? He shook his head. This was what he got for buying a big old house out in the backwoods.

After four minutes of hunting around for the source of the leak he gave up. Time to call the professionals. With a sigh of resignation he went back up the stairs, barefoot this time, and got the Tonawanda Yellow Pages from the bottom of the kitchen cupboard. He'd meant to throw it out lots of times but kept forgetting to put it out in the recycling bin. Good thing he hadn't.

He called the first plumbing service that popped up on the page. All-In-One Plumbing and Interior Decorations. Strange combination, but who was he to judge?

"All-In-One, may I help you?" The slightly nasal voice of a woman echoed into the phone.

"I have a flooded basement," he said. "Could you send a plumber over right away, please? I'm at sixteen twenty-nine Old Spruce Lane."

"Wow," the woman exclaimed. "The old Sullivan place. I didn't know somebody was living there now. Seen any ghosts in the house?"

"Pardon me?" Surprised by her question , Jake's tone was cool. Who was this woman, anyway? He hadn't called for a chit-chat.

"Oops, sorry. Just a moment, please." The woman must have put the receiver down because her next words were slightly muffled. "Sam, Alvin's stuck in Niagara Falls today. Can you run out to the old Sullivan place?" She was back on the line within seconds. "Sam will be there in twenty minutes," she said. "Just look out for the All-In-One truck."

Jake thanked her then hung up. Twenty minutes. Good enough. The damage was already done. What was another twenty minutes worth of water? His indoor pool had probably been collecting for days.

Within eighteen minutes of the call there was the rumble of a truck pulling up in the driveway. They were punctual. A good sign. Jake was on his way to the front door when the bell rang. "Coming," he said, but before he'd gone another five steps the guy was ringing the bell again. "Hold your horses," Jake called out, slightly annoyed. It was a big house. Did they expect him to get from one end to the other in seconds?

He flung the door open, still frowning, and froze in surprise. Instead of the burly plumber he'd expected he found himself staring into the wide brown eyes of a sweet-faced young woman.

He stood there, shocked, then realizing he was staring he cleared his throat. "You're with All-In-One Plumbing?" he asked then looked past her at the big white truck.

"Yes," she said, her voice sweet and mellow and deeper than he had expected. It was a soft, husky voice. Sort of sexy. "We got a call that your basement is flooded."

"And you came with Sam?" He glanced at the truck again but there was no-one in it. The plumber must be at the back of the truck offloading the equipment.

The girl laughed, a soft, rippling sound that brought his eyes back to her. "I'm Sam," she said and held out her hand. "Samantha Fox, at your service."

This was the plumber? Jake almost laughed out loud. They'd sent him a pretty little thing with long dark hair pulled back, her heart-shaped face rosy and cheerful. And at her feet was a toolkit. She probably was the plumber, after all.

He took her hand in his and was surprised at how soft it was. Definitely not the hands of a plumber.

She was a dainty little thing, dressed in denim work shirt, jeans and heavy work boots. She looked like a child trying to play grown-up, dressed in daddy's work clothes. All-In-One

Plumbing had sent a kid to do a man's job. He was looking forward to seeing how that would work out.

He felt a tug and that was when he realized he was still holding her hand. "Oh, sorry." He let go then stepped back. "Come on in."

"Thank you," she said with a smile, seeming unperturbed by the fact that he'd just been holding her – or at least her hand – captive.

She bent and picked up her toolkit and stepped past him and into the foyer, pulling work gloves out of her pocket as she went. "Point me to the basement," she said with a tilt of her head.

It was when she stepped in that he realized that her hair swung all the way down her back, teasing her pert little bottom. He tore his eyes away before she turned and caught him staring. Jesus, what was wrong with him? Was he so starved for the sight of a woman that he couldn't help ogling this one?

So he hadn't been out in a while – a long, long while – avoiding the public as much as possible, even ordering his groceries online. Still, that didn't meant he should react this strongly to the first woman to cross his threshold. He shook his head. This was definitely not like him and he'd better get a hold of himself if he knew what was good for him. There was no room in his world for a woman, no matter how attractive she was.

"It's this way," he said and led her down the hallway toward the door. He switched on the light and went down the stairs with Samantha – or Sam as the woman at the office had called her – in tow.

As they stopped at the bottom step she looked up. "Hmm, I see what's going on." She sat on the second to last step and proceeded to loosen the laces on her work boots. "I have a feeling this is all connected to your water heater," she said as she pushed the boots off and pulled off one sock and then the other.

She had small, delicate feet with pink-painted toenails. Nope, definitely not the feet of a plumber. Jesus, he was staring again. Jake tore his eyes away and stepped past her and down into the water. "You're probably right," he said, adopting a nonchalant tone. "I was checking around that area but couldn't find anything. Maybe you'll have better luck."

"I'm sure I will," she said with a chuckle, "because I know what to look for."

She stepped into the water behind him and then she was wading past him toward the huge white cylinder around which the water lapped. "This is a very old model," she said, and ran her hand along the top. "You're probably going to have to invest in a new one."

She ran her hands all the way down the sides, probably checking for leaks, then bent over to peer at the pipes running into the cylinder.

And that pert bottom he'd glimpsed upstairs? Now he was treated to a full view of it. Dang!

"Found it," she said, head still down and butt in the air. "Your pipes are really old, probably the original ones that came with the house. These ones definitely need to be changed."

She straightened her back and rested her hands on her hips. "But don't worry. I can give you a temporary fix." She gave him a sympathetic smile. "I know it can be difficult doing major repair work, especially when you haven't budgeted for it. I can change the washer down here and the coupling up there. That should buy you some breathing space." She shrugged. "A few months, maybe, but that should give you some time to plan for the major work. Redoing the piping in this old house is going to take some doing."

He nodded. She was going to change the washer, she said. He'd love to see her do that. With her soft hands there was no way she'd get those rusted pipes loose.

She waded back to the steps and got a wrench from her toolkit then pulled on her work gloves. "I need you to turn off the main so I can get started."

"The main?" He stared back at her, feeling stupid. Now where the heck was this main she'd asked about?

She cocked her head to one side. "You do know where it is, don't you?"

Defeated, he shrugged then gave her a rueful grin. "Nope. Sorry."

"No problem," she said. "I'll get it. I've worked on so many of the houses in this neighborhood I can make a pretty good guess where it is." She waded to the back door and climbed the couple of steps then shoved it open. She was outside for less than a minute when she called out, "Found it. It's off now."

When she returned she picked up her wrench again and advanced on the water heater. After she'd clamped the nut with the device she pushed. It didn't even budge.

Jake stepped forward. "Let me –" he began but she put up a gloved hand, cutting him off.

"Step back, please," she said, her voice firm. "I don't want you to get hurt."

"Uh huh," he said sarcastically, then was just about to step forward and pluck the wrench from her hand when she swung it up, making him jump back. She'd almost brained him with the thing.

She brought it down and gave a surprisingly gentle tap to the rusted pipe. "Loosens up the rust buildup," she said with a quick grin. After hooking the wrench onto the nut again she pushed. This time it turned without a fight. Water gushed out then stopped, giving her free access to the pipes. She stuck her finger in and pulled out a rubber washer, so worn and cracked that it was crumbling in her hand. "The guilty party." She held it up then rested it on top of the water heater. She pulled a new washer from her pocket and within a couple of minutes she'd inserted it and was tightening the pipes with a brand new nut.

"This one's all set." She raised her eyes to the still dripping pipe above. "I'll have to get my step ladder for that one."

Before he could offer to help she was back up the stairs and through the door, leaving him standing there in the water. Talk about a bundle of energy. He shook his head then trudged up the stairs in her wake. Proficient or not, she'd need help with that stepladder.

Jake soon came to realize how competent a plumber Sam was. Within thirty minutes of first entering his house she had fixed both pipes and had used the sump pump to clear the water from his basement. With all the water gone the damage was clearly evident – sodden carpeting, a soaking wet sofa, and boxes of books that had sucked up the water like sponges. He would have to dump the whole lot, including the book he'd gone looking for.

"Looks like you're going to need a lot of help," Sam said as she surveyed the damage.

Jake grunted, not at all happy with the prospects before him. He knew he needed help but he was not enthused with the idea of having strangers trudging through his house. As his eyes wandered over the mess he folded his arms across his chest and gave a deep sigh.

"I'm not doing anything tomorrow. I'll come back and help, if you like."

His head jerked up and he turned to look at the woman who, toolkit in hand, looked ready to leave. "Why?" He frowned and looked at her with suspicion. Was she some sort of Good Samaritan?

She shrugged. "I told you, I'm not doing anything tomorrow." She didn't wait for a reply but slipped past him and headed up the stairs.

Was she leaving? She hadn't even been paid.

"Yes," he called out to her disappearing back.

She stopped at the top of the stairs and leaned against the door jamb, looking down at him. She tilted her head. "Yes?"

"Yes." Then he added grudgingly, "Please. I would appreciate the help if you can make it."

"Of course," she said cheerily. "I can be here by ten o'clock but now I have to run. I have to go put on my interior decorator hat."

"Hang on a second." He climbed up the stairs behind her. "Let me grab my check book."

A couple of minutes later, check in hand, Sam headed out front where she climbed up into the truck and perched on the edge of the seat. It looked like she wouldn't be able to reach the pedals otherwise. She started the engine and then gave him an infectious grin and a wave. "See you tomorrow," she called as she backed out of the driveway.

He almost grinned back at her but caught himself just in time. Instead, he nodded then watched as she drove away.

· · ❧ · ·

"HI, SWEETIE. THAT was quick." Alvin Fox was coming out through the front door just as Samantha drove in. "Meg told me you'd gone out to the Sullivan place so I thought you'd be there for a while."

"Nope," Sam said as she swung her toolkit out of the truck and walked toward her dad. "Just a couple of leaky pipes. Nothing good ole Sam couldn't handle."

"That's my girl," Alvin said and leaned down to receive the kiss she was aiming at his cheek.

She deposited the toolkit on the ground beside their feet then straightened and folded her arms across her chest. "That job was nothing compared to the work that still needs to be done. That place is a mess."

"Water damage?"

"Among other things. The whole basement needs to be cleaned out and the rest of the house...let's just say it needs a major overhaul." She shook her head. "Looks like since the Sullivans left the current owner hasn't even had a chance to furnish the place."

"There goes the interior decorator in you." Alvin chuckled. "Next thing I'll hear is that you're over there fixing the place up. I know you."

"Uhmm, well…" She cleared her throat. "I'm going back there tomorrow morning."

Alvin narrowed his gaze. "Don't tell me you convinced the family to redo their entire house?"

"I plead not guilty." She put up her hands in protest. "All I did was offer to help clean the mess in the basement. And from what I could tell it wasn't a family. It was just…a guy." She frowned even as she said the word. He hadn't been the type you'd classify as a 'guy'. He was all man, and a serious-looking one at that.

"A guy, huh?" Alvin put his hand to his chin and looked thoughtful. "A guy all alone in a big old house on the outskirts of town. And I should let my little girl go out there to help him clean up?"

"Dad, I'm thirty-two years old. Not exactly what anybody would call a little girl. And besides, he's not like a biker kind of a guy. He's actually quite mature." She tapped a finger against her chin. "I'd guess…late thirties, maybe even forty."

"Ah, haa," Alvin said, drawing out the sound. "I see." He gave her a look of amusement.

"Dad, it's not like that," she said, quickly defending her position. "It's just…he seemed so distant. Almost…sad. Like he needed a friend, you know?"

"And, of course, in steps my little Samantha, always ready to befriend the friendless." Alvin gave a sigh but it was lightened by his understanding smile.

"I just want to help, Dad." She gave a shrug, picked up her toolkit and headed into the office. "I'm heading out to Mrs. Roach's place. I'll give you a call tonight, okay?"

Alvin called his goodbye to her and then she heard his truck roar to life. She'd ended the conversation a bit abruptly but she'd had to. She hadn't been completely honest with her father and, much to her annoyance, she had one of those faces that could never hide a secret. If she hadn't moved she would have been turning pink in a minute.

The truth was, there was more to her offer to help than she'd let on. The moment she'd laid eyes on her new customer she'd felt an attraction that had almost knocked the breath out of her. Oh, she'd done a great job hiding it behind her super cheerful act and competent 'plumber girl' exterior. But today, out there at that big old house, she'd felt something she hadn't felt in a long time. A very long time.

After a hiatus of four difficult years she, Samantha Fox, had met a man who'd begun to kindle the dormant embers of her heart. And he wasn't wearing a wedding ring.

THE BILLIONAIRE BROTHERHOOD

THE BILLIONAIRE BROTHERS KENT

Book 1 - The Billionaire Next Door
Book 2 - Babies for the Billionaire
Book 3 - Billionaire's Blackmail Bride
Book 4 - Bossing the Billionaire

THE CASTILLOS

Book 1 - Beauty and the Beastly Billionaire
Book 2 – Training the Tycoon
Book 3 – The Mogul's Maiden Mistress
Book 4 – Eva and the Extreme Executive

HOLIDAY EDITIONS

Rome for the Holidays (Novella)
Rome for Always (Novel)

The NAUGHTY AND NICE Series

Volume 1 - Naughty by Nature

COMEDY, CONFLICT & ROMANCE Series

Book 1 - Taming the Fury
Book 2 - Outwitting the Wolf
Book 3 - Romancing Malone

THE BILLIONAIRE BACHELORETTES OF BEL-AIR

Book 1 -In Bed with the Enemy

NOVELLAS

The Billionaire's Bold Bet
Tamed by the Billionaire - The Sequel

MADE FOR THE MOVIES

Trading Spaces

Back from the Future

COLLABORATIONS

A is for Arrangement – Eden Adams

INTERNATIONAL

SPA - Domado por el Multimillionario
FRE - La Milliardaire Apprivoisee
SPA - Romance de la Criada en los EU
FRE - En Amour avec la Femme de Chambre
GER - Vom Milliardar Gezahmt
SPA - La Novia Cautiva del Multimillionario
SPA - Engano Peligroso
JAP - For titles in Japanese, contact Tuttle Mori
Agency, Tokyo

NONFICTION

How to Write a Romance Novel

COLLECTIONS

THE BILLIONAIRE BROTHERHOOD, Coll. I - Vols. 1 - 4

THE BILLIONAIRE BROTHERHOOD, Coll. II - Vols. 5 - 8

THE BILLIONAIRE BROTHERHOOD, Coll. III - Vols. 9 - 12

BILLIONAIRE BROS. KENT - Books 1 - 4

THE BILLIONAIRE BROTHERHOOD DOUBLE COLLECTION - Vols. 1 - 8

THE BILLIONAIRE BROTHERHOOD MEGA-COLLECTION - Vols. 1 - 12

THE BILLIONAIRE BROTHERS KENT - Vols. 1 - 4

THE CASTILLOS - Vols. 1 - 4

COMEDY, CONFLICT & ROMANCE - Vols. 1 - 3

HOME for the HOLIDAYS - Vols. 1 - 3

AUDIO BOOKS

Available from your favorite retailers and libraries

Tamed by the Billionaire

Maid in the USA

JUDY ANGELO

Billionaire's Island Bride
Dangerous Deception
Bedding Her Billionaire Boss
Her Indecent Proposal
So Much Trouble When She Walked In
Married by Midnight
Rome for the Holidays
Billionaire's Blackmail Bride
How to Write a Romance Novel

. . ❧ . .

Author contact:
judyangeloauthor@gmail.com

. . ❧ . .

TO TAME A TYCOON

For updates on books,
and my 'Pay It Forward' Charity Program,
visit
judyangelo.blogspot.com[1]
USING MY BOOKS EACH MONTH TO SUPPORT A
WORTHY CAUSE

---

1. http://judyangelo.blogspot.com/

Did you love *To Tame a Tycoon*? Then you should read *Daddy by December*[2] by JUDY ANGELO!

A little girl, a wish, and a woman determined to stay out of his reach. How to reconcile the three?

Billionaire investor, Drake Duncan, is at the top of his game. He decides to hire a ghostwriter to work on his memoir. Little does he know that the writer who will answer the call is truly a ghost - from his past.

Meg Gracey is the proverbial 'starving artist', a writer down on her luck. When she is offered a contract as ghostwriter she jumps at the chance, only to later realize that the job will throw

---

2. https://books2read.com/u/4Azwpb

3. https://books2read.com/u/4Azwpb

her directly in the path of the man she vowed never to 'touch with a long stick'. Caught between starvation and emotional torture she is forced to choose.

Does she follow reason or give in to the desires of her heart?

Read more at judyangelo.blogspot.com.

Also by JUDY ANGELO

Bad Boy Billionaires - Where Are They Now?
Tamed by the Billionaire - The Sequel

Billionaire Bachelorettes of Bel-Air
In Bed with the Enemy

Billionaire Brotherhood
The Billionaire Brotherhood III, Vols. 9 - 12

Historias Multimillionarias para Navidad
Rome para Navidad

KNOWLEDGE in a NUTSHELL
How to Write a Romance Novel

MADE FOR THE MOVIES Fantasy Romance
Trading Spaces
Back from the Future
Back from the Future with BONUS Trading Spaces

Multimillonarios Machos
Domada por el Multimillionario
Domado por el Multimillionario, Bilingual Version

The BAD BOY BILLIONAIRES Series
To Tame a Tycoon
Sweet Seduction
Daddy by December
To Catch a Man (in 30 Days or Less)
Bedding Her Billionaire Boss
Her Indecent Proposal
So Much Trouble When She Walked In
Married by Midnight
Bad Boy Billionaires - Collection II, Vols. 5 - 8
Bad Boy Billionaires Mega-Collection Vols 1 - 12

THE BILLIONAIRE BROTHERHOOD
Tamed by the Billionaire (Roman's Story)
Maid in the USA (Pierce's Story)

Billionaire's Captive Island Bride (Dare's Story)
Dangerous Deception (Storm's Story)
The Billionaire Brotherhood Coll. III Bks 9 - 12
The Billionaire Brotherhood Collection I, Vols. 1 - 4
The Billionaire Brotherhood Double Coll. Bks. 1 - 8

The Billionaire Brothers Kent
The Billionaire Next Door
Babies for the Billionaire
Billionaire's Blackmail Bride
Bossing the Billionaire
The Billionaire Brothers Kent

The BILLIONAIRE HOLIDAY Series
Rome for the Holidays
Rome for Always
Home for the Holidays

The Castillos
Beauty and the Beastly Billionaire
Training the Tycoon
The Mogul's Maiden Mistress
Eva and the Extreme Executive
The Castillos - The Collection

The Comedy, Conflict and Romance Series
Taming the Fury
Outwitting the Wolf
Romancing Malone
Comedy, Confict & Romance - The Collection

The Naughty and Nice Series
Naughty by Nature

Standalone
The Billionaire's Bold Bet

Watch for more at judyangelo.blogspot.com.

About the Author

New York Times & USA Today best-selling author, Judy Angelo, considers herself a 'traveling writer'. She currently resides in Ontario, Canada but prior to that she called New York and then Illinois home. She has also spent considerable time in the Caribbean, Latin America and Europe. She loves to travel as it provides her with interesting and diverse settings for her stories.

Judy fell in love with romance novels as a teenager and has never lost her passion for these stories of love and life, conflict and reconciliation, relationships and family. For her, it was a natural progression from reading romance novels to writing them. So far, she has written over 70 romance novels, including the best-selling Bad Boy Billionaires series. Her other series include The Billionaire Brothers Kent, The Castillos, and the Comedy, Conflict & Romance series.

She hopes to continue entertaining her readers with intriguing stories for many years to come.

Website - www.judyangelo.blogspot.com

I would love to hear from you! judyangeloauthor@gmail.com

Read more at judyangelo.blogspot.com.